"How did you  **Dawn's birth**

Andy shook his he   wn came into my life?"   ooked across at the baby dozing on her mother's lap. "Forget the magic on the mountain on New Year's Day?" he said softly, and his words brought back the serenity of that morning.

Then he leaned across and kissed her cheek, and Montana knew he really did remember that day with emotion. "You were amazing."

She found herself leaning toward him. His long fingers stroked her jaw and drew her closer. Just the feel of his warm strength splayed across her cheek and the caress of his thumb sent sensations tumbling into her stomach and chest, and she couldn't help but close her eyes. Montana didn't see his mouth coming, but she'd known it would happen. Wanted it to happen.

Dear Reader,

The best things often come to you in dreams. A year ago I dreamed up a town in southeastern Queensland called Lyrebird Lake. The lake, the townspeople and the legend of the lyrebirds that live there took hold of my imagination. Lyrebird Lake is a place of wonder, and those fortunate enough to be touched by lyrebird magic are changed by it forever.

The lyrebird is a native Australian bird with a lovely harp-shaped tail that he uses to attract his mate. With the ability to uncannily mimic any sounds, the lyrebird mesmerizes the Australian bush. In Lyrebird Lake, a myth surrounds this clever scrub dweller—that he can heal the past, and bring new love to a bruised heart.

In this series you will meet three wonderful midwives, all mothers-to-be, as they settle in to work at the new midwifery center of Lyrebird Lake. Will the lyrebird magic touch these women and the men they are destined to meet?

Enjoy Montana's story—my first book of the trilogy—and may you, too, be touched by the magic that is Lyrebird Lake.

With warmest wishes,

Fiona McArthur

THE MIDWIFE'S LITTLE MIRACLE
Fiona McArthur

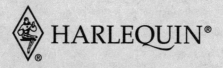

TORONTO • NEW YORK • LONDON
AMSTERDAM • PARIS • SYDNEY • HAMBURG
STOCKHOLM • ATHENS • TOKYO • MILAN • MADRID
PRAGUE • WARSAW • BUDAPEST • AUCKLAND

Recycling programs
for this product may
not exist in your area.

ISBN-13: 978-0-373-06685-8
ISBN-10:   0-373-06685-6

THE MIDWIFE'S LITTLE MIRACLE

First North American Publication 2009

Copyright © 2009 by Fiona McArthur

www.eHarlequin.com

Printed in U.S.A.

THE MIDWIFE'S LITTLE MIRACLE

Dedicated to Flora May Simpson.

The best mother-in-law, who just laughs
at the mess in my house.

CHAPTER ONE

NEW YEAR'S morning began with the faintest hint of grey shimmer on the horizon and Montana gently stroked her fingers across her swollen stomach.

This had been the first New Year's morning without her husband and the last she would spend at the mountain house before the new owners moved in.

The sea was a long way off, somewhere below the white fluffy quilt thrown over the mountains, shrouded like the future she couldn't see but did have faith in.

Eagle's Nest Retreat sat so high and wild that it overlooked everything and Douglas had loved it when he'd painted here.

The sky had lightened only enough to illuminate the deep drifts of mist in all the lower valleys across from the house, and she sat symbolically alone, and accepted it would always be so.

The first contraction squeezed gently, like the tendrils of dewed spider webs that stretched the tops of the stumpy grass, and she nodded when she felt the mysterious child within herald her intentions.

Montana had agreed with her two best friends that, for her child's sake not her own, it would be safer to avoid the mountains for the last two weeks of her pregnancy.

So it wasn't Montana's fault her baby had decided to come earlier.

She closed the house and gathered her shawl and water bottle and, grasping the rail on the stairs, made her way slowly down to her vehicle. To actually climb into the four-wheel drive proved much more difficult than she'd expected and she chewed her lip as she started the engine.

The chug from the diesel engine scared a flock of lorikeets into flight, a little like the flutter of apprehension she fought down while she waited for the engine to warm up. Two more waves of pain came and went in that time.

As the contractions grew closer and fiercer a tiny frown puckered her forehead. It might not be as easy as she'd thought to drive the truck for two hours in early labour.

After thirty minutes of careful navigation down the misty mountain sweat beaded her forehead and Montana's breath fogged the windscreen with the force of the pain. Though still focussed on what lay around the next corner she found it more difficult to divide her thoughts between road and birth.

The dirt track twisted and turned like the journey

her baby would make within her and on an outflung clearing overlooking the mist-covered valley she had to pull over to rest and shore up her reserves.

A pale grey wallaby and her pint-sized joey stood at the edge of the clearing and their dark pointy faces twitched with fascination at her arrival.

Montana's labour gathered force and she glanced with despair at the distance to the valley floor. It was impossible to descend the mountain safely when she couldn't concentrate on the road and suddenly the tension drained from her shoulders as she slumped back.

So be it.

When the pain eased she slid from the truck and spread a rug on the damp grass and tucked her shawl and water beside her. She eased herself down and sat with her arms behind her to watch the deepening of the horizon from coral to pink to cerise as the sun threatened to rise through the cloud below.

When the next surge had dissolved she sighed and gazed skywards. Maybe he was looking down.

'You should be here, Douglas.' A single tear held her loss that still pierced so keenly.

She felt the whisper of cool breeze brush the dampness on her cheek and suddenly she was not alone and she didn't care if she imagined him because the next pain was upon her and she needed his strength with her own to stay pliant on the waves of the contractions.

I am here, the wind whispered. *You are safe.*

I love you, she heard, and then she listened to the nuances of her body and in her mind she watched the descent of her baby and squeezed her husband's hand and the waves changed in tempo and direction and strength and suddenly the urge was upon her to ease her baby out into the world.

The sun cascaded through like the gush of water, her baby's head glistening round and hard and hot in her hands, and then the next pain was upon her. Her baby's head rotated towards her leg and the released shoulder slid down and through to follow.

In long, slow seconds, her baby's body eased into the world until, in a waterfall rush, legs and feet followed and in a tangle of cord and water and fresh broken sunlight, her baby was born.

The unmistakable sound of a newborn's first cry startled the birds as Montana reached down and gathered her daughter to her, forgetting the cord that joined them, and she laughed at the tug that reminded her that all umbilical cords were not long.

A daughter. Douglas's daughter. She turned, not expecting to see him yet so grateful she had imagined him in her time of greatest need.

The clearing was empty save for the mother wallaby and her skittish joey, and like the last of the night tendrils they too disappeared silently as the fog rolled away.

She shivered.

* * *

'You must be Montana?' His voice was different from Douglas's, not as deep or careful with enunciation, but the same timbre of quiet authority and caring drifted over her and that must have been why she didn't jump.

She wound down the window and saw the darkest auburn hair and green eyes that proclaimed his relationship to her friend. So this was Misty's big brother from Queensland. He towered over her door.

It seemed almost normal that Misty's four-wheel drive had pulled up next to hers in the morning light and have this man stand beside her car door to look in.

He had to bend down quite a bit to her level and she smiled to herself at the trials of tall men. 'Yes, I'm Montana. I gather Misty sent you?'

He nodded. 'I'm Andy.' He looked across at the top of her baby's head snuggled into her chest with blankets over both of them in a big mound, and he smiled.

To Andy they both seemed so peaceful despite the absolute isolation in which they'd met. There was something so tranquil about the mother and daughter in this isolated spot that it was difficult to grasp she had given birth without support. 'And who is this?'

Montana smiled and he felt the curve of her lips and the softening of her eyes right down to his combat boots and back up again where heat flickered in his chest like a hot coal from an outback campfire.

'This is my daughter, Dawn,' she said, and her serene voice wrapped around him like the fog he'd just passed through to get here.

'Hello, Dawn.' He smiled at the thatch of dark hair against Montana and the baby snuffled as if in answer. 'I can guess what time she arrived.'

His smile faded and his training reminded him this woman had been without assistance. He framed the question as delicately as he could. 'Any problems you need help with?'

She glanced at him and he felt the humour behind her voice more than he heard it when she spoke, and the observation confused him. Since when had he picked up fine distinctions in tone from unknown women?

'No, thank you, Doctor,' she said. 'Third stage complete and I'm not bleeding or damaged. My baby has fed.'

He didn't like the way he was so conscious of his sister's friend but maybe that was because he felt for her recent loss.

He knew he avoided emotions these days, had done for three years. It was the way he'd decided to stay and he empathised with her journey. But, actually, he was more than conscious of her.

They were on the side of a mountain, for heaven's sake, and she'd just had a baby.

He concentrated on the things he was good at.

'Right, then. Let's get you out of here.' He glanced around to decide where to reverse the vehicle.

Montana's voice was gentle, as if explaining to a child—and a slow one at that. 'We have to wait for the fog on the road to clear further down before we go.'

He could feel himself frown but what could she expect? He hadn't predicted resistance to rescue. 'I managed to get here.'

'That's lovely.' And she smiled that damn schoolmistress smile again that made his neck prickle under his collar.

She went on. 'I'm not risking my daughter in a drive down the mountain with a man I don't know until the mist is gone completely, even if the man driving does rescue for a living.'

The inflexible set of her chin and the tilt of her fine-boned face should have exasperated him but inexplicably he could feel himself bend like a reed to her wishes. So be it. 'Fine. We'll wait.'

He paused while they both pondered how long that would be. 'Would you like a cup of tea?'

He saw her eyes widen as her taste buds responded and his own smile twitched as he tried to contain his amusement. Ha!

Deadpan, he gave the choices as he watched her face. 'Earl Grey, breakfast, peppermint or jasmine tea?'

A tiny frown marred her forehead as if she wasn't sure if he was joking. 'Jasmine?'

'Fine. I'll rustle that up shortly.' He pulled the hot water bottle his sister had slipped into the car from the pocket of his doctor's bag and showed it to her.

'Misty sent this.' He touched the handle of her car door and raised his brows again. 'May I?'

When she nodded he tucked the warm rubber bottle under the blanket against her feet.

He couldn't help noticing she had little feet. Slim, shapely ankles, too, but he liked her feet. He heard her sigh with the warmth as he stepped back, and that dragged his mind away from her toes. Now he had a foot fetish? What was wrong with him this morning?

The air seemed colder now that he'd moved back away from her. 'Sure you're warm enough? I have a great heater in the car.'

She tugged the blanket closer around her neck. 'That seems sensible. Perhaps you could heat your car first and then I could hand you Dawn to keep snug while I do a bit of a tidy with myself?'

Nurses. Obsessed with being tidy, he thought. He grinned. 'I'll be right back.'

She watched him walk away. A tall, lean man, even taller than Douglas. She really had to stop comparing people to her darling Douglas. Andy resembled his sister uncannily but there was no doubt he held the Y chromosome. It had been kind of him to come, unnecessary but kind.

No doubt Misty and Mia had panicked when

she hadn't arrived last night but she'd wanted one more night on the mountain before she had to move out to start afresh.

The most important night, as it turned out, and she smiled down at her daughter.

Minutes drifted peacefully and then he was back. 'The car is heated. Shall I take Dawn?'

He held out his arms and she saw he'd unwrapped a small blanket and a tiny warm beanie from another hot-water bottle.

It didn't surprise her any more about his sister's intuition. Misty was known for her premonitions. 'Misty must have been pretty sure Dawn would arrive.'

Andy nodded. 'She rang me at five this morning in a state and I've learnt to believe her when she "feels" something.'

'Is it a family trait?' Montana could see he was proud of his fey sister. She'd found another thing she liked about him.

He smiled crookedly and the way he curved his firm mouth made him more a real person and less Misty's brother. 'Sometimes I'm accused of uncanny intuition if we're searching for someone, but not with the precision and clarity of Misty.'

He pulled the soft bonnet over Dawn's hair as if he'd beanied a baby many times and then rolled her little body in the blanket as he peeled her away from Montana's skin so that the cold air wouldn't distress her. Dawn didn't even whimper.

Montana was quietly impressed with his confidence with her newborn daughter—even Douglas, an obstetrician, hadn't been that adept at handling babies. The thought was diverted by a sneaky eddy of cold air that had whispered against her own skin like a blast from the refrigerator, and she pulled the blanket in tight and hugged it with a shudder.

Andy wrapped Dawn in another warm shawl and tucked her against his chest as he flattened the blanket back firmly around Montana with his other hand. He must have seen her shiver.

Dawn whimpered and he whispered softly to her. His cheek rested against her tiny head with his skin on hers to comfort her while he carried her to the warmth of the car.

Montana frowned at how at ease they looked together and decided she'd had enough huddling to keep warm while she waited for the mist to lift.

Her heated feet felt good and she slipped the bottle up to tuck into her now loose trousers and keep her stomach warm as she pulled her shirt together where she'd opened it to keep her daughter snug against her skin.

The sheer bliss of hot water to wash her face and hands made her smile and after she'd communed with nature she crossed to Andy's car and her daughter.

Andy had the cup holders out on the dashboard and each held a steaming cup of tea that caused puffs of condensation on the windshield above each mug.

Dawn dozed quite happily tucked into Andy's arm and Montana stilled him with a raised hand as he went to lean across to open the passenger door.

She slid in. 'Don't move. She's settled.' He looked remarkably at ease for a big man with a newborn in his arms.

She inhaled the aroma. 'The tea smells wonderful,' she said, and gathered the cup in both hands to divert her mind away from him. The heated comfort infused into her hands like the flavour had into the water.

How brilliant that Andy had instinctively known not to fuss. Even Douglas would have flapped and scolded at the thought of Dawn's arrival here on the mountain, and Montana sipped her tea slowly and relaxed.

They sat silently for many minutes and Montana may even have dozed.

When she opened her eyes again he was looking at her. Not staring, just an appraisal to see if she was fine. She couldn't remember when she'd felt so comfortable in a stranger's company.

'Were you frightened?' His words were soft and acknowledged something powerful and amazing had happened on the mountain that morning and she took pleasure in his lack of censure. She smiled at the bundle that was her daughter and shook her head.

Suddenly it was important he understand that she wasn't reckless with her daughter's life. 'It was the most serene dawn. I couldn't drive any more, not safely anyway, and when I stopped it all happened as it should.'

She paused thoughtfully and then went on. 'I won't say I was lucky it all went well—because I have always believed a woman is designed to give birth without complications. I was just not unlucky, as some women are.'

Andy pondered her statement. That seemed a bit simplistic for him but it wasn't his job to dispute her views and instead he flattened his chin against his chest and squinted at the baby snuggled like a possum into him. 'What do you think Dawn weighs?'

Montana looked proudly across at her daughter and smiled again. 'Maybe six pounds. Say two and a half thousand grams. She's three weeks early but she's vigorous.'

'She's perfect.' Like her mother. The glow that infused him with that thought surprised him but he refused to examine the reasons. The occasion was special enough for odd feelings.

'I know,' she said. They smiled at each other in mutual admiration for Montana's baby. This time Montana was the first to look away and he wondered if she too had become aware of that ease between them, which was unexpected.

He reached over the back of the seat and lifted a small lunch holder. He needed to be practical, not fanciful. 'Would you like some sandwiches? Misty made some with egg and some with ham. We could put them together and pretend it's a Sunday break-fast.'

'Actually, I'm starving.' Her face lit up and he enjoyed her eagerness for food. No doubt his plea-sure came from a primitive male-provider thing but he could fix her hunger when he'd let her down by not being there half an hour earlier.

She unwrapped the sandwich and bit into it with small white teeth and with obvious relish. Labour must be hungry work, he thought, and the glow inside him flared a little more.

'Is there anything you don't have?' she said just before the next bite, and the words were strangely prophetic.

Someone like you, perhaps? Whoa, there boy. He was getting way out of his depth here and he needed to pull back urgently. He looked out at the mist below them in the valley.

His voice came out a little more brusquely than he'd intended but he couldn't help that. 'I don't have a trailer to bring your truck down with us—but I'll come back and get it later for you.'

She saw the mist had begun to dissipate lower down the mountain.

Soon this interlude would be over, she'd be tucked up in a ward bed with Misty and Mia fussing over her, and everything would be as it should be, except Douglas wouldn't be there.

All the things she hadn't said and now couldn't share with Douglas were irretrievable and she needed to accept that. But she dreaded each day in her normal environment, which had become so entrenched in loss and memories.

Her husband wouldn't be in the maternity ward where she'd first seen him. Wouldn't be in any of the familiar places where they'd both spent the last years of his life.

How did one cope with this feeling of desolation? Or of the guilt-ridden feeling that Douglas had let her down somehow by dying? What of the fact that a stranger had been the first man to see Dawn and not Douglas?

Her eyes stung and a tear rolled down her cheek. 'I don't want to go to the hospital. Actually, I don't ever want to go back there. I don't even want to go back to my house in town, which is ridiculous as I don't have the energy to organise a clean break. I have no idea how I am ever going to go back to work there.'

She bit her lip and then shook her head. 'This is not like me. I'm sorry. I have no option. Ignore what I just said.'

The understanding in his green eyes nearly triggered the tears again. 'Anyone would think you'd had a big morning,' he said, and the compassion in his voice told her he understood. He really did understand.

Andy slid his arm across the seat and around her shoulder and it was as if he encased her in empathy.

Despite the fact that she didn't know him, it felt good to be hugged. Incredibly good.

'It must be hard without your husband,' he said. 'I felt the same when my wife died.'

He saw she knew his story. Misty would have told her. He hoped she hadn't told her how he'd almost gone off the rails.

'It's harder than anything in the world,' she said, 'and sometimes I'm almost angry with him for leaving.' Montana lifted her face to his. Her eyes shimmered with loss and he remembered that too.

'I remember that feeling,' he said.

He squeezed the fine-boned shoulder under his hand and she responded to his understanding and told him.

'The first of May. It was an aneurysm. There was no warning. Douglas went to bed smiling and never woke up. He was thirty-five and didn't even know he would be a father.'

Andy didn't rush in with condolences because when his wife had died he'd hated that. The silence lengthened as they both reflected on their losses.

Finally he said, 'It was a tragedy. Though he has given you a beautiful daughter and he will live on through her.'

She nodded. 'I know. But I don't ever want to hurt like that again.'

Andy sighed. Amen to that. Time was a great healer—he knew that from bitter experience—but the early years were painful and something he'd promised himself he'd never do again. She had to do it with a daily reminder in a child.

It was good he had a direction in life with the hospital now. She needed something like that.

Andy squeezed Montana's shoulders once more and then let his arm drop. 'I'll get your things and put them in my car.'

'I want to go home. Not to the hospital.' The pain was stark in her voice.

He'd suspected that was coming. 'Fine. I'm sure your own personal midwives will arrive as soon as they hear you are home.'

He smiled and Montana found she could smile back. He was right. Of course she didn't have to go to the hospital. Mia and Misty would make sure she was fine.

CHAPTER TWO

ANDY spent the week of his holidays doing three things.

First, he accumulated extra operating hours as a locum surgeon for the occasional disaster that cropped up at the lake to ensure his skills remained current. You never knew when a casualty would arrive without time for transfer to the base hospital.

Second, he lost no opportunity to promote the idea of transfer to Lyrebird Lake for any health professional who would listen and might be remotely interested in relocating.

The Lake needed staff if it was to move into the new era the mine would bring, and this was a great opportunity to scout for potential colleagues.

Andy had sworn he would do his best to help find staff. If he didn't, the hospital would be downgraded even further and the funding diverted to the base hospital eighty kilometres away.

That would happen over his dead body.

And the third thing he did was try not to think about Montana Browne.

His was a busman's holiday that allowed him to catch up with his only sister once a year and not intended for relaxation or dalliance.

Since Montana's baby had arrived early he'd spent a lot of time in and out of Misty's friend's house after work because Misty had taken on the cooking and shopping role for Montana in some pre-arranged, pre-birth deal the girls had going.

The other friend, Mia, had been assigned washing and garden work so Andy had offered to mow the lawns before he left.

He didn't mind. It gave him a chance to watch Montana, a pastime he suspected he could become captivated by.

Something wasn't right with Montana today.

It was a typical three-women-and-extra-brother afternoon at Montana's house and he found it all strangely poignant that it was the last he would be present at.

Misty stroked Dawn's downy cheek as she whispered to the tiny baby in her arms. 'You are beautiful. Yes you are.'

Andy heard his sister's crooning but his attention was on Montana as she rested back in the lounge with the cup of jasmine tea he'd made for her and fielded the barrage of questions Mia seemed obsessed with.

'You sure you didn't mean to have Dawn up

there in the mountains all the time? You must have known you were going into labour? Didn't you have a premonition?'

'No premonition. I leave that to Misty.' Montana's quiet voice drifted across to him and he saw her glance at him but she didn't smile.

Why did he need her to smile? 'And to Andy,' she finished, and he savoured the way she said his name.

He should go. Get out of this hens' party and think about packing to head home. He still had a heap of shopping to do before he flew back tomorrow morning and if he went back to the Lake without the special ingredients Louisa, their housekeeper, had requested, he was a dead man.

He just couldn't seem to tear his eyes away from Montana today—though that was nothing new. The day he'd met her replayed like a favourite movie in his brain.

He could still see her alone in an isolated clearing on the side of a mountain surrounded by mist—a woman as calm and tranquil as a Tibetan monk—after giving birth alone.

She'd declined hospital assessment even though he admitted she had two willing experts in his sister and Mia.

Here in her own home, even with her new baby, he'd never seen her succumb to any sort of anxiety, until now.

He kept remembering how serene she'd been

when he'd first arrived to bring her back. That serenity was missing, and he didn't think it was just the fact that Mia was hounding her again, but maybe it was.

'Mia, leave her alone.' Although he said it quietly, his voice cut across the room and the three women turned towards him.

Dawn began to cry and Misty carried her across to her mother as she glared at her brother. Andy smiled.

All three women could indicate displeasure with their eyes but his sister won hands down. Their mother had been the same but Misty would have been too young to remember that.

'Sorry. I didn't mean to startle everyone. Forget it.' His sister would flay him for upsetting the baby but he was more worried about upsetting Montana.

Maybe his sister could help. 'Can I see you for a minute, Misty, please?'

Misty shrugged and Montana raised one eyebrow mockingly as if to say he'd picked the wrong household to assert his authority, but he could see she was fine with him at least.

Misty approached with that militant look in her eye and he turned away with her so the other two couldn't see their faces.

'Sorry.' Diversion might be a useful deflection. 'Just wanted to ask you if you think it's a good thing Montana stays here when it obviously makes her so sad.'

As a spur-of-the-moment diversion it had come with a lot of thought.

Misty frowned and tilted her head as if to peer inside his brain. He hated it when she did that because a lot of the time she could guess what he was thinking, and he didn't even know what he was thinking himself.

'What choice does she have?' She spoke slowly as she watched him and he tried his own attempt at peering. She probably thought he was interested in Montana. Well, he was—but not like that!

He'd been there when Montana had said she didn't want to come back to this house, this town, anywhere near the hospital.

'Montana could come back to Lyrebird Lake with me and work in the hospital when she's ready. She said she didn't want to go back to Westside. We're still looking for a midwife and an evening supervisor. Maybe she could fill those positions until she decides what she wants to do.'

Misty was still peering. 'You'd have to talk to her about that yourself. And how would you get her there? She hates small planes.'

He didn't like the scepticism in Misty's voice but she didn't seem as negative the more she thought about it.

She shook her head but again not as convincingly. 'I can't imagine Montana wanting to uproot herself from Douglas's house and head to the back of beyond with a new baby.'

It wasn't that dumb an idea. He frowned as he watched his sister consider the idea.

Too bad if she didn't agree. It was Montana he needed to convince. 'People in South East Queensland live there with babies. There's no strangeness in that,' he said.

Misty screwed her face up in disbelief that he could be so obtuse. 'There is the problem of leaving everyone you know at a time you need them most.'

He'd be there for her and so would the others. 'She'd know me. There's a town full of people who would help.'

'Strangers!' Misty's scorn came out a little forced and he began to hope she'd seen some advantage for Montana in his suggestion.

He lowered his voice. 'Maybe that's what she needs right now.'

Montana drifted across the room towards them and he watched her approach. Misty looked pointedly at her brother. 'Ask her.'

He grimaced. It wasn't how he would have chosen to broach the subject but something told him Montana had got the gist of their discussion anyway and maybe postponing this wasn't helping. Even from the beginning he'd never doubted her powers of observation.

At least her expression could be construed as interested, not wary. Here goes, he thought. 'I wondered if you might like a change of scene, Montana.

Maybe a job when you're ready, up my way. We have vacancies we can't fill at the cottage hospital.'

She watched his face as he spoke and he hoped he made sense. 'I think I've mentioned I live in a rambling old house with tons of room. There's another semi-retired doctor plus any locums that can come for a week or two to give us relief.'

He glanced briefly at the bassinet by the window, where Dawn now slept. 'You and Dawn could share with us for as long as you like, or even have your own cottage as there are a few on the hospital grounds if that would suit you better.'

She looked more receptive than he'd hoped for so he went on. 'We're looking for another midwife and an evening supervisor. Misty told me you have a management certificate and I thought you might be interested in a fresh start.'

'Don't blame me,' Misty said, but both of them ignored her as Montana considered the idea.

Obviously Misty expected Montana to turn him down but if he wasn't mistaken he'd say Montana actually looked relieved he'd asked her.

She certainly seemed interested. 'I've heard you say you don't deliver babies at the Lake,' she said quietly, and raised her finely arched brows. 'Is that hospital policy or just because of the lack of midwives?'

'Occasionally we have babies. There's myself and Ned, the semi-retired GP I live with, but we only have one midwife on staff with any obstetric experience. We catch unexpected babies when we have to but send on the rest to the regional hospital because that's where the skill base is.'

Of course that would be where her interest would lie, he thought, and wondered how he could turn that to his advantage.

'That is something we expect might have to change as the town grows.' He shrugged and grinned. 'So if you can convince a few of your friends to migrate north, that would be good, too.'

He picked up on her interest and began to experience the exhilaration he usually only felt when he'd accomplished a difficult surgery or diagnosed an elusive condition. Or landed a beautiful fish.

'A midwifery-led clinic and case load, you mean?' Her head was up and he could feel her intensity.

He just might have her. 'Perhaps, though you'd have to explain caseload midwifery more fully to me some time. I know you've been involved with the stand-alone centre at Westside.'

She nodded. 'Women-centred care is springing up more commonly now since women consumers have documented what they want. I would be happy to clarify the concepts for you.'

She chewed her bottom lip. 'How long would I have to stay if I came out and just had a look?'

She was still cagey but he could feel she was close to considering his offer and he pressed his advantage, unable to believe his luck.

'No ties.' He didn't want to scare her off, for a

variety of reasons. Once she'd seen the place and the potential he'd seen, she'd be hooked. He hoped. She had a lot to offer and Matron would be delighted.

'We could say you're visiting, if you like, then if you decided to go home no one would be any wiser.'

'A freeloader?' She wasn't happy with that and he doubted she'd ever taken anything for nothing.

'With a view to helping us out in the future. That's not freeloading. Rest for as long as you need. A month or two at least. Lots of things run on a barter system at the Lake. We'll sort something out. It's not easy to get staff so if you stayed to work short or long term, we'd be fine with that.'

'Babysitting?' She'd changed. He couldn't pick when it had happened, but she'd lost the anxious look she'd had all morning. Now she was efficient and focussed. He could see that and he liked it. It was beginning to feel as if they were the only two in the room and he liked that as well—perhaps a bit too much.

He thought of Louisa, his housekeeper, and how much she'd adore Dawn. 'Our housekeeper is a grandmother whose grandkids live away. She'd be in seventh heaven with Dawn and would happily look after her when you needed her to.'

Overall, after his explanations, Montana appeared relieved, if anything, and he began to believe it could possibly happen. Why did it matter so much that this woman would come when others he'd been philosophical about hadn't?

'Thank you for asking me,' was all she said. 'I'd like to think about it.'

He watched her exchange a look with Misty and his sister frowned. Was that a good look or a bad look?

He opted to give them time to talk in case he went backwards from here. He'd done all he could. He nodded and moved across to apologise to Mia.

Montana watched his progress across the room before she turned to Misty.

She needed this. The memories everywhere she looked were crushing her. 'I'd like to go with your brother to Lyrebird Lake.'

Misty frowned. 'You made that decision fast.' But the lack of surprise in her friend's voice made Montana smile.

She sighed ruefully. 'I've been a mess, trying to decide whether to ask him all morning. I knew they had staffing problems but it will be weeks before I'll want to think about work. With somewhere to stay, it's the perfect answer.'

'Perfect answer to what?' Misty said.

Montana heard the censure and could see Misty did not understand her rationale.

'You have everything here,' Misty went on. She included Mia in an encompassing gesture. 'You have us.'

Too true, Montana thought, and that part would

be hard. 'I love you guys, and I will miss you, and that will be the hardest part, but there's too much here.'

She met Misty's eyes. 'I need to get away and start life afresh with Dawn. I'm not looking to replace Douglas, just looking for somewhere everyone doesn't panic about what to say to me in case they upset me. I'll never forget Douglas, can't imagine being with another man, but I need to be a whole person for my daughter, and I can't do that here.'

'Fair enough, but don't decide immediately.' Misty hugged her. 'He leaves tomorrow. It's going to happen fast and you might wake up and wonder what you've done.'

Montana looked across at Andy, where he was laughing with Mia. He made her laugh too, and that wasn't an easy thing to do. 'I know. But that's a risk I have to take. I would be in safe hands. Will you help me?'

'Of course.' Misty sighed and glanced at her watch as she tried to calculate how much time they had. 'You never know. I might turn up for a visit there one day by myself.'

'You'd have to bring Mia, and her boyfriend wouldn't like that—he'd have to cook for himself. But we'd have fun.' The two women smiled.

When they left the next day it took Montana a while to come to grips with the fact that not only did

Andy own the plane but he would be the pilot if she wanted to avoid a two-day car trip with a newborn.

She'd always had a reluctance to fly and the idea of a tiny two-seater plane with her daughter was right up there in nightmare territory. If she hadn't had that unexpected confidence in Andy that she'd felt from the first moment she'd seen him, she would have pulled out.

She eased herself stiffly into the cramped seat, quickly breathed in and out a couple of times and tried to secure her seat belt, but it wouldn't latch into place. Her fingers fumbled with it.

She could do this. She tried again one-handed with Dawn against her chest and then again with slightly more desperation until the door beside her opened and the woodsy aftershave she'd begun to associate with Andy drifted past her nose.

'May I?' He looked down at her with a reassuring smile and she remembered why she'd decided to go with this man.

She sighed and relaxed, and at her nod Andy clicked her belt and then secured the tiny strap around Dawn that threaded between mother and daughter like a leather umbilical cord for emergencies.

It meant she was joined again to her daughter and she liked the idea for the flight.

She wondered who would be drawing reassurance from whom in the coming flight. Thank God Andy was there to look after both of them.

Then Andy climbed into the other side of the

plane and squeezed his big frame down next to her, and she could feel the warmth from his body like a soothing shield. She enjoyed feeling slightly safer until she remembered his presence meant they were close to take-off.

Oh, boy, she thought grimly, and concentrated on his strong hands as they caressed the controls. An unexpected wish to feel those fingers squeeze her hand in comfort made her twist to stare out the window.

'You OK?' She heard his voice and she turned back and hoped her face at least appeared calm.

'Fine,' she lied, and he looked across at her and grinned.

He nodded and resumed his flight preparations. She chewed her lip while he talked to the flight control tower and then it was too late to change her mind because the little Cessna had begun to taxi in an ungainly rattle down the runway.

Another small plane in front of them awaited take-off and she watched in sick fascination as it lined up and then hurtled away from them down the runway before it climbed precariously away into the sky. She swallowed the fear in her throat. Their plane would have to do that.

She wished irrationally that Dawn would be less settled and whimper or do something to distract her, but her daughter snoozed on regardless.

Andy positioned the plane and the engine built in noise until it seemed to scream—a little like the noise Montana wanted to make but couldn't—and her nerves stretched.

He looked across at her and flashed his white teeth in the joy of the moment before take-off. Pretty impressive dentistry, she acknowledged, by grimacing back, then she returned to the only thing she could do as she breathed in and out. She prayed.

Breathing was a good thing and improved the lightness in her head at least, and praying could be helpful if divine intervention was required.

He released the brakes and the plane began its thunder down the runway and when she risked a look the tarmac beside her blurred. Suddenly the noise changed and her stomach plummeted and she realised they were in the air as the ground dropped woozily below her window.

OhmyGod. She turned her head away and closed her eyes.

Obviously Dawn travelled better than her mother. She was asleep. Montana tried to think of something different that rhymed with doom and gloom and boom. She moistened her lips and risked opening one eye.

They'd levelled out and Andy looked pretty relaxed. She opened her other eye.

She'd talk about the weather. 'So, do you have emergency supplies in this thing and a homing beacon?' That wasn't what she'd meant to say.

Andy smiled. 'GPS tracker and, yes, we have basic emergency supplies. Today we even have English muffins, ginger marmalade and Norfolk punch as extras for my housekeeper and jasmine tea for you. But despite the size of the plane, we're safe.'

He glanced at her sleeping daughter. 'Dawn isn't worried.'

Montana looked down at her. 'Hmm. She has less imagination than I have.'

'Wimp.'

His eyes danced and she noticed he had little brown flecks through the green of his irises, then she frowned at the unfairness of the comment.

'Hey, if I was a wimp, I wouldn't be here.'

The hundred-watt smile he sent her way warmed the ice around her heart and made her forget she and Dawn were in a fragile capsule a mile above the earth. Now it felt more like she floated in the air without support amongst the clouds outside her window. Heady stuff. Probably oxygen deprivation.

'That's true. You are not a wimp. Well done.' His words continued to warm that cold spot she'd had in her chest for far too long, though it was probably just reactionary euphoria that they hadn't died on take-off.

He changed the subject and began to recite anecdotes about the older doctor he lived with, and by the time they were nearly there she had acclimatised to the concept of flight, with Andy at least.

Montana's first sight of Lyrebird Lake was as they broke through the low cloud and saw it lying ahead.

The grey of the water on the lake reflected the grey of the clouds that had dogged most of their journey and suddenly it suited her mood and her spirits plummeted.

She didn't know anyone in this town except Andy. No doubt this sudden low feeling was helped by residual pregnancy hormones, but what had she been thinking of to leave everything she knew behind and literally take off with her week-old baby and a man she'd barely met? Even if he was the most restful man she'd ever known?

What if it didn't work out? What if Dawn cried every night and kept the whole household awake? What if she lost this rapport with Andy that she relied on so much?

CHAPTER THREE

'YOU still with me?'

Andy could feel the change in Montana even though she tried to hide it.

He was way too aware of this woman but everything he'd done to try and change that awareness hadn't worked and he did need to ensure he had a safety line to draw between him and her.

He was more than happy to help when he could, but it didn't mean he had to try and fix all her problems.

It could be just her distrust of flying—lots of people weren't comfortable in small planes—and he admired the way she'd overcome that fear without fuss or demands. But he had an idea it was more than that.

She was independent, he was that way himself so that shouldn't bother him, but he wanted her to know he was available as a shoulder to lean on. As a brother, of course.

Actually, he wanted to reach over and squeeze

her hand and reassure her that everything would work out but despite the way his sister and her friends hugged each other, he didn't feel at ease in the touchy-feely set. Not platonically anyway.

Then there was the suspicion that once he'd touched Montana it might be hard to stop, and Andy struggled with that idea of touching another woman after Catherine.

He'd brought Montana here for a job—he really did respect all the things she'd achieved in the past if what Misty said was true—and it was her administrative skills he needed.

He was better unencumbered with love and family and he didn't doubt Montana could be the whole package—if he let her, which he wasn't going to. He was better alone. He'd promised himself that and he had too much baggage to inflict on someone else.

He watched her slender fingers slide gently over Dawn's hair and wondered who drew comfort from whom as she cuddled her baby close.

'I'm OK,' she said. 'I just had a minute of panic.'

She stared out the window at the expanse of water below and he leant across to point things out because it directed his thoughts away from this uncomfortable space he was in at the moment.

Besides, he'd always loved this view and he hoped she could see the beauty below despite the scar of new development near the lake.

A scattering of established houses along the

shore added to the town which nestled under a set of hills. 'See the hills and the lookout. We have great bush walks and even a waterfall up there.'

Then the hospital came into view. 'That's all in the hospital grounds.' He pointed out the largest tin-roofed building and a scattering of smaller buildings spreading out from it. 'The one across the park is our house.'

Montana inclined her head towards the town below. 'The town is smaller than I anticipated.' Her voice seemed smaller than before, too, and a moment's panic had him hoping she didn't want to turn around and go home.

'It's tiny compared to Westside but it's a full of good people in a good town.' He wanted her to feel comfortable and realise the potential he saw in the area himself. The hospital needed her. She had nothing to do with his own needs.

'We have a large feeder district but anyone with a complicated medical condition would still be shipped out. Admissions to the hospital are fairly simple and mostly brief. Same goes for births. If it's not simple, it's gone. But if we expand our services, that would change with the needs of the mine population.'

She nodded. 'Lyrebird Lake is an unusual name. Is it because of the shape of the lake or because you have lyrebirds?'

He'd never seen a lyrebird. 'I guess it's the shape of the lake. We're pretty far north as a habitat.

There's not much rainforest around here, though we do have some patches of wet forest which would make it possible.'

She nodded. 'They are supposed to look like a small turkey with a tail. Has anyone ever seen one here?'

'Not that I know of.' He shook his head. 'I've heard some pretty strange noises in the bush so I guess I could have heard one. Apparently the lyrebird can copy another bird's song, or an animal, or even man-made noises like chainsaws and crying babies.'

She smiled. 'That would be a mother's nightmare. One crying baby is enough.'

'Ned says there's a local myth that those who have suffered will be rewarded when the lyrebird visits. No visitations for me in the three years I've been here, and I think he's pulling my leg.'

She smiled at his sceptical amusement. 'So why are you here?'

He shrugged. 'Lyrebird or not, the Lake healed me, and I think it could help you too.' He looked across at her and hoped she realised he genuinely believed that and not just because he could use an extra midwife in the hospital.

'The people are legitimate, as is their need, and you can't stay immune to their warmth,' he said. 'I appreciate that after living in the city.'

She nodded so maybe she did understand. 'Which hospital did you work in?' she asked, and for the first time in a long time he didn't mind answering.

'The year after my wife died I spent in the emergency department at Sydney General. U and O they called it—understaffed and overwhelmed.'

His voice lowered as he remembered. 'You know what it's like. Extremely long hours, no emotional involvement with patients, just save them or lose them. I was happy to do that as I built up a big wall to hide behind. I couldn't see myself becoming more clinical and distanced from humanity.' He shook his head.

'Misty, and the friends I had alienated, saw it.' Rueful grin there at the memory of how taciturn he'd been since his wife had died. 'They ganged up on me and suggested I resign. Then told me about Ned, the Lake's retired GP, and how he needed help for a few months. He's got degenerative vision failure and I've been here ever since.'

He thought back over the last couple of years and how his mindset had altered for the better. 'I've grown to love it here and I'm committed to providing the medical needs of the community. If those needs adjust then the hospital will darned well adjust too.'

He pointed to the north. 'It made things interesting when the mine opened up twenty kilometres away and now the farmland is selling faster than the local government can subdivide. We have our first restaurant in town.'

'A real restaurant in town? Very flash.' She smiled, probably at the pride in his voice, and he laughed.

'It is for us.' He'd take her there one day. Angelo would love Montana.

He went on. 'The hospital will get busier and the idea of a midwifery-led unit is not as far-fetched as you might imagine. There is a core of women in town who are very progressive and well read on their rights. They'd love women-centred care.'

She tilted her head. 'And I thought you were just saying that to tempt me.'

He smiled and tried not to think about who was tempting whom, because that wasn't part of the plan. 'Now, why would I do that?'

She looked at him thoughtfully. 'I don't know. Perhaps you recognised my symptoms from your own past or maybe…' She paused and considered him. 'You just wanted someone else to have the headache of setting up a new service.'

He grinned. 'Bingo! We could be a good team.' He adjusted the flaps on the wing. 'You ready? We're going in.'

The noise of the plane engine changed and the little cabin tilted as they began their circling descent.

Dawn squirmed against her mother as her ears blocked from the altitude change. Montana slipped her little finger into her daughter's mouth so she would suck and swallow and pop her ears.

As a diversion from the risks of landing small aircraft, Montana mulled over what Andy had said.

He seemed a little obsessed with the hospital and the town, and he lived with an older doctor and his housekeeper. Obviously he'd been devastated at the loss of his wife and now devoted himself to his work.

But what about friends? Or other women?

Didn't he have a life?

Did he expect she'd be as committed as he was because she'd lost her husband too? Was that why he'd been so keen to have her come?

Maybe he'd planned to staff the hospital with bereaved doctors and nurses.

All good questions, she told herself.

She had to smile at her fanciful meanderings but they were coming in and the thoughts helped to divert her mind away from the ground looming up at her.

She hadn't guaranteed she'd stay at the Lake and she might not feel the same next week. 'I hope this works out as you plan. That Dawn and I can settle for a while.'

In the few seconds before he answered Montana realised that as the pilot he was responsible for the safety of their descent.

What was she thinking? Now was not the smartest time to distract the pilot.

'Please, ignore me and concentrate.' There was a squeak of sheer terror in her voice and he looked across at her and smiled reassuringly.

'I've done this hundreds of times.'

She grimaced at him. 'Why does that not reassure me? You only have to blow it once in a plane.' She'd tried for lightness and she wasn't sure she'd pulled it off, but he returned to her previous statement and his relaxed example helped her hands unclench.

'I know there are no guarantees you'll love the Lake like I do,' he said. 'That's understandable. We'll see what the next few weeks bring.'

They landed smoothly and taxied up to park near a tin shed that proclaimed a welcome to Queensland and Lyrebird Lake, and Montana thought how she would have felt welcome anywhere that had firm earth beneath her feet.

As they waited for the propeller to stop revolving Andy slid his hands onto his strongly muscled thighs and turned to grin at her. 'Well, you survived your flight and here we are.'

'Thank you for getting us here safely.' Her comment was heartfelt. 'Interesting airport.' She looked around at the deserted tarmac, though there did seem to be some activity in a hangar across the grass.

Andy followed her gaze. 'There are great people in the flying club out here. I'll have to bring you out to one of their barbeques. It's a fun evening under the stars with a bunch of larrikins.'

He inclined his head towards the hangar. 'Though they do take their flying seriously and I can't beat one of them in the flour bombing.'

The propeller swung on its last rotation and

Andy flicked the last of his switches and then climbed out to come around to her side.

He opened her door and warm air rushed in and wrapped around her like welcoming arms. She hoped it was prophetic. She hadn't expected to feel like that about the new town.

Andy reached in to undo the strap around Dawn and Montana's seat belt, and the release of the restraint seemed almost symbolic of her new life.

'Here,' Andy said. 'Give me Dawn while you climb out.'

Dawn whimpered when she was lifted but settled happily on Andy's shoulder and Montana was reminded how at ease he was with her daughter.

He used his other hand to help steady her as Montana climbed awkwardly over the doorframe but soon her feet were thankfully on the earth again. She resisted the impulse to bend down and kiss the ground, but it wasn't easy.

His green eyes sparkled with mischief and she had the sneaking suspicion he knew what she'd been thinking.

'This way,' he said. 'My car is in that shed and it's too hot to leave you both out in the sun while I get it. We'll walk across and I'll drive it back to the plane for the gear.'

He shifted Dawn down his chest so he could cover her head from the sun and the glare, and she loved the way he did these little things so naturally.

She couldn't help but wonder how Douglas

would have handled having a baby in his life twenty-four hours, seven days a week, as children hadn't been high on his list of priorities.

Surreptitiously she watched Andy lope across the grass beside her and she strained to hear his one-sided conversation with Dawn.

'You're a big girl now, Dawn. Did you enjoy your first flight? You were very brave. You must be Mummy's daughter because she's very brave. You are going to love it here.'

I hope so, Montana thought, because she had the feeling that Andy would do everything in his power to look after them and help them settle. If only she didn't feel disloyal to Douglas it would be all good because she couldn't help feeling as though she had the opportunity of fresh beginnings here.

As they drove through the town Montana felt even better. The main street was so wide it had huge shady trees planted in the middle of the road and the cars were parked at an angle next to the footpath.

People waved at Andy as he drove and the whole atmosphere was one of enjoyment of life. The buildings were old but restored in heritage greys and blues and she smiled across at Andy who delighted in her obvious enjoyment.

Like the flight had been, settling into Lyrebird Lake proved much easier than she'd anticipated, and Andy was the person who made it so.

The first morning Montana came in to breakfast

Andy was there with a welcoming smile and a cup of tea. 'Your jasmine tea, *madame*.'

He looked very pleased with himself as he handed her the cup. 'Perhaps I could cuddle Dawn?' He tilted his head. 'If that's OK with you?'

Dawn had been a little upset overnight, no doubt picking up her mother's unsettled mood, and she guessed Andy must have heard her.

Her stomach dropped. 'Did she keep you awake?'

Andy's forehead crinkled. 'No. I only heard her for a couple of minutes all night so you must be an awesome mother,' he teased, and Montana relaxed.

She'd thought the walls seemed pretty thick. Still, it was weird to suddenly share a home with people she barely knew, and she couldn't help worrying that her new baby would disrupt the household.

Andy had his hands out so she passed Dawn to him and sat down as her daughter semi-grimaced at Andy. 'Typical. That's the first smile I've seen all morning. She likes you all right.'

'What have you done to your poor mother, missy?' Andy admonished Dawn with a teasing finger. Then he glanced across as if to assess Montana's fatigue.

'Take it easy today,' he said. 'If you're up to it, we'll go for a walk along the lake this evening so you know the lie of the land. Otherwise you should be sleeping when Dawn sleeps.'

He was sweet. She'd said the same thing herself to countless women. 'Who's the mother here? It's strange to have someone say something to me that I'm always telling other new mums to do.'

'Funny that,' he said with a lopsided grin. 'Ned is always telling me I coddle my patients.'

When Andy went off to the hospital the house seemed very empty, although Ned and Louisa made sure she had company if she wanted it and encouragement to rest when she needed.

Ned, while supposedly semi-retired, was a white-browed, hyperactive Scotsman who bounced from one task to another with boundless energy.

He ran a clinic every afternoon in a rundown set of consulting rooms at the end of the house, played chess on Tuesdays and Thursdays and was the local Rotary Club president. For fun he carved native animals out of driftwood from the lake and the house was bedecked with his figurines. Sadly, he found it harder with his decreased eyesight for fine detail.

He hobbled a little with his stiff hip, and if he misplaced his glasses—which he did frequently— he could barely read the brand name on the cereal pack, but his diagnostic skills were in no way diminished by his eyesight.

Intuitive and caring, Ned saw through Montana's façade of calmness and she found herself sharing more with him about her loss of Douglas and her struggle to move on from it than she had with either of her womenfriends.

She wondered if Ned had been equally as

healing with Andy. Maybe Ned was the lyrebird that brought healing.

Ned's housekeeper, Louisa, was a round Yorkshire dumpling of a woman with merry eyes and big breasts that Dawn cuddled into like a pillow from the first moment.

The feeling appeared mutual as Louisa would commandeer Dawn whenever she could and whisk her off to the kitchen to watch while she cooked.

The first evening Montana glanced at the clock to check the time more often than usual, until she realised she'd begun to calculate the time until Andy returned.

It was probably only because she had more time than she'd expected on her hands, although that didn't account for the little skip in her heart rate when he did walk in.

In fact, he looked so attractive with his easy smile and laughing green eyes when he asked about her day that she couldn't help her own smile in return.

She glanced across at Louisa and Ned, who seemed to have faded into the distance since his arrival and weren't paying attention to her and Andy. 'I haven't achieved anything. They won't let me help.'

'Dawn looks happy.' He glanced at the couple, who laughed as they peeled vegetables together. 'No discontent there. You must have achieved something. Come for a walk before tea.'

A walk in the cool of the evening did sound heavenly, Montana thought, and no doubt Dawn would enjoy an outing in the fancy old pram Ned had procured from somewhere.

But surely Andy didn't need to go out again. Selfish woman, she admonished herself. 'Don't you ever sit down? You've just come in.'

Andy shook his head. 'I relax better upright. I'd enjoy it, too.'

After some organising of the pram, the three of them meandered along the lakeside path under overhanging trees, and the cool evening breeze was as delightful as Montana had imagined it would be.

They walked side by side and she had to be careful not to lean too close towards Andy as they strolled. It was probably just the fact of two people out walking with one baby but it almost felt like a family excursion. That was ridiculous when she'd only known Andy a week.

The houses they passed all seemed to be built of heavy timber and pretty gables and wrought-iron enclosed back verandas that looked over long rear gardens.

If this was suburbia then Montana hadn't seen anywhere like it as peaceful or pretty, and the warmth of the evening seemed to wrap the three of them in contentment.

She felt like a child peering through other people's windows at Christmas, which was strange when in Westside she had her own house and garden, but suddenly home felt a million miles away from here and not a quarter as attractive.

'Do you ever think of buying a house around here?' The words fell out and she hoped they weren't too personal, but Andy didn't seem worried she'd asked.

He smiled across at her. 'I might do some time in the future. I did buy my dream block of land at the end of the lake, but most of my time is spent at the hospital or on home visits.' He shrugged.

'At the moment I wouldn't be able to give a house and garden the care they needed until more medical relief arrives.'

Montana wondered if that was really true, or did Andy choose to spend so much time finding things to do so he didn't have to be alone in a house of his own?

They meandered on and the sun set behind the hills as they turned back towards the doctors' house.

The three weeks left in January passed in a blur with what became ritual walks along the lake in the evening and caring for Dawn through the day.

Late in the month Andy took Montana to the flying club for a barbeque and she followed him nervously out of the car.

Andy was greeted like a long-lost friend and he introduced Montana to Paul, the local flying instructor.

'So do you fancy learning to fly, Montana?' Paul asked with sweep of his hand towards the sky.

'Not at the moment, thanks,' she said, and glanced

across at Andy whose laughter-filled eyes dared her to tell Paul what she really thought.

'You'll have to come up with me one day,' Paul said, oblivious to the shudder from Montana. 'Andy's only an amateur in a baby plane.'

He pointed to a petite brunette serving salad at the trestle table. 'My wife has a beautiful biplane, a Tiger Moth. Now, that's real flying.'

Driving home later, Andy teased her about her not taking up Paul's offer.

'I can just see you with goggles and a flying jacket in the front of the Tiger Moth.'

'Not.' Montana refused to take the bait. 'But thanks for taking me out. It was lovely to have a change of scenery and, you're right, the flying club mob are larrikins but lovely.'

Montana had begun to itch for some work, an occasional relief shift even at the hospital when Andy told her about a staff member off sick, but Andy insisted Montana relax and enjoy Dawn while she settled into motherhood.

It was like stolen time and Montana had never done so little for so long. Despite some reflex ennui, she felt more at peace than she had since Douglas had died.

She realised the gnawing pain from her loss of Douglas had been eased by her love for Dawn and the warmth from her housemates and, of course, the ever-caring presence of Andy. Her calm persona became the real Montana, not just the projection.

February saw Montana drift to the surgery end of the house and glance over the list of patients. At least she could see if there were any nursing tasks she could do for Ned, like occasional dressings or injections or even minor suturing.

She began to spend an hour or maybe more in the surgery but as the days passed more clients began to be allocated in her time to drift in. Soon the time had stretched from one hour and then two.

Montana discussed with Ned the need for a well-women's clinic and the idea to use her women's health certificate for the first time in years gave her the incentive to scan the internet for health sites to update her knowledge.

One morning she realised she'd been there six weeks already and Andy had seemed to have fallen into a routine of including her in his day.

He arrived in the kitchen and swooped on Dawn who lay propped up as she stared fascinated at the world from her pram while Montana ate her breakfast.

'Would you like to come for a turn around the garden, gorgeous, before I sit down for my break-fast?'

Dawn's little face lit up as soon as Andy entered her vision and she had even begun to coo when he picked her up. Montana realised that she wasn't the only person falling under Andy's spell. Dawn adored him.

Her own external relationship with Andy hadn't changed since she'd moved into his house but she wished she could say the same about the way she reacted to him emotionally.

To Montana he was unfailingly polite and supportive and she had to admit she looked forward to seeing him in the mornings but there was still a certain reserve between them that wasn't there for Dawn or the others.

But, then, he was everyone's favourite.

Louisa he teased unmercifully, and the affection in the scoldings she gave him showed how much she enjoyed their exchanges, while Ned treated Andy as his favourite son.

Apart from breakfast and their evening walks, Montana actually saw very little of the workaholic Andy.

As she watched Andy bear Dawn away Montana decided the less she saw of Andy the better. She'd come to suspect her panicked misgivings during the plane trip could have substance. Following Andy out here could be detrimental to her peace of mind. Then there was the fair lashing of guilt over her faithlessness to Douglas.

To her dismay she'd begun to daydream about Andy. He appeared in her thoughts and snippets of new memories would have her drift into a reverie when she least expected it.

Both he and Ned treated her like a princess, opened doors, pulled out her chair, stood when she entered the room. It was totally different from her life with Douglas, who had loved her but had expected almost the opposite.

Douglas had been the prince, the doctor and the artist, and she the person responsible for the mundane tasks of day-to-day living as well as all nurturing and household business.

Here Louisa managed the house, Andy the hospital and Ned the clinic. Montana looked after Dawn and learnt about Lyrebird Lake.

She knew Andy suspected she still missed the day-to-day interaction from her husband—or maybe that was what he had missed the most when his wife had died—but she wished he wouldn't try to replace that because she found it harder to picture Douglas's face each day and easier to conjure up Andy's.

She didn't feel comfortable to lose the memory of her husband so quickly and easily, and the rising tide of guilt was the only tarnish on her peaceful life.

What she could see even without actually spending much time with Andy was how much the town relied on him.

Ned couldn't suture and had difficulty when he tried to read the names on drug ampoules and bottles because of his diminishing eyesight.

Andy slipped those tasks into his already busy schedule and Montana continued to take on what tasks she could to lighten his load.

Andy dealt with all the hospital admissions and

transfers to the base hospital, minor surgery and emergencies, and apparently worked on the disaster rescue team when needed. She could help.

Late in the eighth week of her stay Montana swung gently on the veranda swing with the warmth and weight of Dawn on her chest, and watched the sun set over the lake.

She'd have to go in soon for tea but for the moment the gentle breeze and cerise reflection off the water were glorious and she felt more energised than she had since Dawn's birth.

The days had begun to drag and she realised she was ready to return at least to part-time work.

The noise of the latch on the screen door behind heralded the end of her solitude and she glanced up from the water.

'Hope I'm not intruding.' Andy raised his brows as if she only had to say and he would go again.

CHAPTER FOUR

ANDY really was the most gorgeous man and she didn't understand why he hadn't remarried and surrounded himself with a brood of auburn-haired children when he was so wonderful with Dawn.

Of course, her daughter seemed as pleased as Montana that he'd joined them. She cooed and smiled at Andy's familiar face and Montana thought at least Dawn would know a little of what a father figure was like when she could have so easily have been devoid of all male company.

Certainly at Westside her daughter would have been in a predominately female environment.

Montana patted the seat beside her. 'Join me. We seem to have very little time to chat. Was there something particular you wanted to discuss with me?'

She edged over to make room for him on the swing and then Andy's woodsy cologne, which almost reminded her of the bottlebrush foliage she'd arranged in the vase today, was there and she realised she'd grown to not only recognise but respond to the aroma of Andy. When had that happened?

His was nothing like the expensive cologne Douglas had preferred but was just as manly— funny how Andy's cologne made her think of unobtrusive strength—which was as comforting as the man it belonged to.

For Andy, he savoured her warmth against him and he realised how much he missed the little feminine aspects that Montana abounded in. She dazzled him as she sat here like the sun that reflected off the lake and yet he could see she had no idea how much he delighted in her company.

He'd been watching her for a while from the lounge and she'd looked so peaceful he'd been reluctant to break into her thoughts.

'Are you settled here?'

'Unless you're planning to evict me, I have no thoughts of moving on. Why?'

He couldn't help but smile at her. 'Fancy a bit of work?'

Her chin went up along with the sparkle in her eyes. 'I was just thinking that.'

Good, he thought, satisfied she was at ease. 'There are a couple of things I want to run by you.'

She turned towards him and regrettably it became harder for Andy to concentrate with her brown eyes on his so expectantly.

He regathered his wits. 'Ned mentioned your well-women's clinic idea. I think that would be great. We could do it when one of us isn't here to give you the other consulting room. Maybe we could run it a couple of hours one morning or afternoon a week?'

'That sounds fine.' Montana nodded.

She looked happy with that, Andy thought, pleased. He hoped she'd be as interested in his next proposal. 'The other thing is that one of my younger patients, Emma, is pregnant and due in July. I wondered if you would be interested in chatting to her about labour and birth over the next few weeks or months?'

'Of course!' Montana sat up straighter and Andy smiled at her passion.

'How old is Emma?' she asked.

He frowned as he thought of Emma and the lacklustre person she'd become in so short a time. 'She's sixteen and about twenty weeks pregnant. My concern is that she's changed from an outgoing girl to an introverted and withdrawn wraith. I know the family well and I'm worried about her.'

Montana's fine brows drew together and he wanted to follow the movement with his fingers and trace them straight again, but this was too important to be sidetracked by fancies.

'Depression, you mean?' she asked.

He concentrated his brain on Emma. 'Yes. I think there's a risk she could become seriously depressed, especially as her mother seems to be going through a low period at the moment.'

The malady of Clare, Emma's mother, still puzzled him. 'I'd like to think with a bit of positive feedback from you, Emma will turn back into herself before she gets used to being miserable. She's only a child.'

Montana raised her eyebrows. 'If she is old enough to become pregnant then she's no child. She's a woman. Make no mistake about that.'

He could see the midwife in her and he knew he'd been right in thinking she would be good for Emma. 'I stand corrected.'

She smiled gently. 'That's my own opinion and Emma's lucky she has you to look out for her. Though if she's only halfway there, she may not want to know about labour and the birth process just yet,' Montana said thoughtfully.

She captivated him. 'Why's that?' He just wanted her to keep on talking so he could watch and enjoy.

'Labour is the last thing a young woman wants to hear about when she's still dealing with the shock of being fertile.'

'Women's intuition?' He was happy to learn. 'What do you suggest?'

She pursed her lips and he was distracted for a moment again as she went on. 'Maybe some sessions on pregnancy health and lifestyle choices? We still have time to engage her for the benefit of baby and her own health. And that information is not so scary initially.'

His brain had become stationary again for a few seconds and he had to blink several times to get his head back together. He kept seeing Montana's mouth and that frozen moment had stunned him silly. He didn't want to go there—or he did and he knew he couldn't—and needed to stay focussed on what she was saying.

'I'm sorry.' He blinked again. 'So you'd be happy to do a couple of sessions with Emma?'

Thankfully Montana seemed oblivious to his mental disorder and he was glad about that. Very glad.

'Absolutely,' she said. 'It might help to ease her into the idea of learning about her body as we go along.'

Everything had double meanings for him at the moment. He fancied a body lesson—specifically concerning the one beside him on the seat—and every day brought more observations for him to store in his expanding folder of what he'd come to realise was growing into a deep and dangerous attraction to the woman beside him.

The mystification had started that first day on the mountain. At least he'd figured out what had been wrong with him a month or so ago and he had the walls up, but he was still struggling to stay focussed when he talked to her. 'So you would be interested in helping Emma?' Damn. He'd already asked her that.

'Yes.' She looked at him as if to remind him they'd been there but there was no doubt in her voice. Forget all that, he told himself. He'd done the right thing in asking.

Montana frowned as she considered Emma's dilemma. 'So how did the parents react to the news?'

He thought ruefully of the intense week he'd had with both sets of grandparents-to-be. 'Badly, but they're coming around. It's even more tricky because Emma's mother isn't well.'

Montana tilted her head. 'In what way unwell?'

Maybe it would help to clarify his thoughts if he ran it by Montana. 'I wish I knew. Clare still puzzles me but there's something niggling below the surface. She had a car accident a month ago and is complaining of being vague, clumsy and ir-ritable, which is unlike her. There's nothing on her cerebral CT scan and I'm not sure but I think I'm closer to working it out.'

Montana nodded. 'More worry for poor Emma. You need your mum at times like this.' She pon-dered that. 'And the baby's father? Is he into rela-tionships?'

'Her boyfriend, Tommy, agrees on keeping the baby, if that's what you mean?' He grinned at scat-terbrained Tommy being a father. No doubt he'd mature eventually. 'I think he plans to stay around, but he's only eighteen. They've been together for three years.'

'You'll be up for a dads' class then,' she said mischievously.

Lord help him, he hadn't seen himself doing that. 'I don't know anything about being a dad!'

'Neither would he so you can both learn as you go along. I could lend you Dawn for an hour for show and tell. You're pretty good with her.'

She was teasing him, and he liked it, but he wasn't pretending to know something he didn't. 'I'll help but you have to come with Dawn.'

'The value will be in the guy aspect. But we'll talk about that later.'

Her eyes shone and felt his mood lift with hers. 'It's not too much work for you to start with?'

'The clinic and Emma?' She shook her head vehemently. 'No. I'd love to help with both of them. I'm starting to climb the walls here without working somewhere.'

'Guilt is good.' He smiled. 'Seriously, though, that's wonderful. I'll set Emma up for later this week or early next week and talk to Ned about the clinics.'

Almost a week later Montana watched out of the lounge room window as Andy's car pulled into the drive.

A too-thin blonde girl—young woman, she corrected herself—had her head down and didn't look up at the house when Andy opened the passenger door.

So he opened doors for everyone. It was such a lovely gesture and it made her appreciate him even more that he would do it for young patients like Emma as well as older adults.

Montana watched the teenager mumble a thank-you and sighed.

She glanced at the table and chairs she'd set up with pamphlets and a gift pack Misty had sent up from New South Wales.

It wasn't so much a statement about learning as information Emma could take away when she left and maybe read at home. But it wouldn't help if she didn't want to be here.

Montana aimed for the whole session to illustrate the fact that a mother's choices affected a baby's future, but none of it would sink in if she couldn't engage Emma's interest.

Montana twitched a tablecloth over the table to create a bumpy but blank face to the room. She'd see if curiosity would encourage Emma's interest later.

Montana moved to the door as Andy ushered in the girl. His face showed palpable relief when he saw her. 'Here's Montana. Montana, this is Emma.'

He looked particularly handsome this morning in his open-necked shirt, and his thick hair was tousled as if they'd had the windows open on the drive. Or he'd been running his hands through it as he'd driven Emma here.

His stressed relief at seeing Montana made her realise for the first time that he wasn't always as comfortable with everybody as he was with her. Strangely that warmed her to him even more.

'Hello, Emma,' she said. 'Thank you, Andy.

We'll sit on the lounge, not at the table, and just chat for a bit.'

Andy tapped the ends of his fingers together a few times and looked hopelessly out of his depth. He stepped back. 'Do you need me?'

Montana took pity on his discomfort and shook her head, although Emma threw him an anguished glance.

Montana smiled at him. 'That's fine. How about if you run Emma home later when we're finished, unless you get called away?'

'Great idea. I'll leave you ladies to it, then, and be back in a little while?'

He dropped the keys onto the bookshelf as if they were hot. 'Emma can give directions if I'm not around and I'll use the utility if I need to go to the hospital.'

Andy waved and backed out of the room. Both women watched him go.

'Well, you really had him scared,' Montana commented, and watched the sudden glint of amusement in Emma's face before she schooled her features into a surly frown again.

Gotcha, Montana thought with an inner smile and a little relief.

She watched Emma perch uncomfortably on the edge of the lounge and share her glances between the door and the floor and tried to remember how it had felt at sixteen in the head's office.

Montana smiled. 'I gather you're a bit nervous about being here?'

'Andy said I had to come.' Emma darted a quick look at Montana and narrowed her eyes. 'I'm keeping my baby.'

So this was the issue. Fair enough, then, Montana could understand her attitude. 'Great. I'm a midwife and I'm a good person to know because I catch them.'

Emma smiled reluctantly.

Montana went on. 'But your baby isn't going to be here for a long time and Dr Buchanan and I thought you might like some extra knowledge to help you in the rest of your pregnancy.'

Montana paused, didn't rush to fill the silence, and waited. The silence lengthened. The relaxed expression on Montana's face didn't change, but Emma began to fidget and finally she looked at Montana.

Emma shrugged. 'So what are you going to talk about?'

'I guess I need you to participate and ask questions otherwise you won't take home as much as you could have. It would help if I knew what would you like to know.'

Emma shrugged again and Montana saw the frightened girl Emma was trying to hide.

'Maybe we should get to know each other before I do all the talking,' Montana suggested. She waited, and Emma eventually nodded.

'You could tell me one thing about yourself, Emma. Tell me about your family maybe.'

Emma stayed balanced on the edge of the lounge with her arms crossed but she did answer eventually. 'There's my dad, who has a sawmill. I get on well with him.'

She looked down darkly at the carpet. 'Or I did before I was pregnant.'

Life wouldn't be fun for Emma at this moment, Montana could see that, and she softened her tone. 'He'll come around. He's trying to adjust the dreams he had—parents have huge dreams in their minds for their children—and now he has to change those pictures into the ones that you will make for yourself.'

Emma looked up and pondered Montana's words before she nodded. This time she met Montana's eyes. 'That does make sense. Thank you.'

That was when that Montana saw the first glimpses of the girl that Andy had spoken of with such admiration so she pushed on. 'Have you any brothers or sisters?'

Emma sniffed. 'Three older brothers who wanted to beat up poor Tommy.' Emma looked up and her chin tilted. 'But I wouldn't let them.'

Montana liked her more every second. 'I have an idea you could be a pretty strong-minded young woman when you want to be.'

Emma rolled her eyes. 'Men are so dumb sometimes.' She shook her head in disgust. 'As if thumping Tommy would help. Tommy's the only one who understands.'

Montana bit back a smile. 'Well, that's a good thing. Lots of younger men wouldn't be able to get their head around being a father.'

Emma even went so far as to grin then. 'I don't think he's even thought of that, just that it's happened, and we are the ones who have to make the best of it.'

'And your mum?' Montana hoped Emma didn't mind her asking.

'Mum's been sick lately.' Emma frowned. 'I am sorry she's had this worry as well but if she'd tried to get better I wouldn't have been away from the house so much and this might not have happened.'

Montana left that statement lie where it fell and moved the conversation around to why they were there.

'OK. Then I'll start with a little about myself and why I think I can help you. I really do know about having babies because that's my job. As a midwife I deliver babies in a hospital and help the mum and baby learn to breastfeed and get used to each other. And I have a baby of my own.'

Emma looked interested at the news of Dawn.

Montana went on. 'I thought we'd talk about pregnancy so you could be comfortable with what will go on in your body as it changes.'

Emma looked out from under her lowered brows. 'So you're not going to try and talk me into not having the baby?'

Montana's gaze locked with the girl's and shook

her head emphatically. 'No. That's your decision, Emma, and it seems to me that you are pretty sure what you want to happen. But with that decision comes a responsibility that you do the best for the baby inside you. Is that how you feel?'

'I suppose so. I know I want my baby to grow healthy, even if it's going to hurt when I have him or her.'

The fear she'd expected was there and Montana nodded. 'Try and remember women are designed to give birth. You're young and young women usually bounce back from birth even better than older women, but we might leave that to talk about another time.

'Did Dr Buchanan tell you we could have another session if you want later? I think there's too much to cover in one day.'

Emma met Montana's look with a sheepish grin. 'He said that. I only came today because he's been so good to me and Tommy, but you're not too bad, so far. I'll probably come back.'

'Thanks,' Montana said, biting back a smile, 'then we'd better get started before I fall out of favour.'

Emma grinned again and the tension lessened noticeably in the room.

'Today I thought we'd talk about where you are in your pregnancy now. How many weeks pregnant are you, Emma?'

Emma unfolded her arms and chewed her nail.

'The ultrasound man at the base said twenty weeks yesterday.'

Montana picked up the book of diagrams she had and pointed to the twenty-week foetus. 'Your baby is fully formed and you should be nearly able to feel his or her movements.'

Emma craned her neck and studied the picture and Montana gave her the book and reached for another copy of the same publication.

'So when are you due?' Montana flicked forward to the picture of a woman with a full-term baby and showed Emma the page number so she could skip forward if she wanted to.

'Andy says the seventeenth of July.'

Montana nodded. 'Right in the middle of the year. So you'll be having a Christmas in July baby. Your best present will arrive some time in our winter, which will be helpful when you are big and heavy for the cooler weather.'

Emma looked up and a faint glimmer of a smile lit her pale face. 'That's the first positive thing anyone has said about my baby.'

Poor Emma. 'That will change. Babies make everyone smile.'

Actually, Emma would be fine. She was smart, would have family support by the end, and was protective of her baby. 'Everyone else is still in shock, honey. Now that this baby is a reality they'll come around. That's what families and good friends do.'

Emma pursed her lips thoughtfully and nodded then settled more comfortably back into the lounge.

Montana sat back in her own chair. 'OK. So let's talk about where your baby is up to now.'

Emma met Montana's eyes. 'It's hard to think of it as a baby. I haven't even got a belly, especially as I threw up so much that I've lost weight.'

Montana nodded. 'For some people that's normal. That should settle now. It's the surge of hormones of early pregnancy and other hormones come more into play now. Just make sure you have something in your stomach before your feet hit the floor if it still bothers you.'

'Like toast. Yuk.' Emma screwed up her face.

'Even a dry biscuit is often enough. But see if you can get someone to bring it to you.' Montana had a sudden vision of Andy bringing the mother of his baby toast in the mornings. If his wife was pregnant, Andy would certainly be the man to do that. She looked at Emma and hoped she had someone to do it for her.

'How about water crackers?' Emma grinned and it changed her whole face. She was in the swing of it now. 'How about a pretzel?' They both laughed and Montana sighed with relief as the young woman within began to show herself more consistently.

'Nothing wrong with a couple of pretzels—just don't overdo it on the salt. It's better for you than losing your breakfast every day.'

Emma stopped chewing her nails. 'Cool. I'll try it and let you know.'

'Just remember when you're eating properly you need to start thinking about making sure you have all the nutrients and vitamins your baby needs because she's greedy to grow and will take all the goodness for herself and leave you nothing if you don't eat enough of what she needs.'

Emma's eyes widened. 'Like a worm?'

Montana smiled. 'Sort of. Right now she's a tiny baby the size of a big banana, about two to three hundred grams. In two weeks she'll put on another one hundred and fifty grams—that's near a pound in the old measurements. She'll grow from around six and half inches long to about eight inches at twenty-three weeks. That's the size of a small doll.'

'Wow.'

Montana nodded. 'It's pretty impressive. Everything is made in miniature and over the next twenty weeks will double in size, which means she…' Montana paused and smiled. 'Notice I call your baby a girl only because mine was.'

Emma nodded with a shy smile of her own and Montana went on. 'Her brain is growing really fast. Mothers need to know that what they eat, drink, smoke or expose themselves to—for example, I wouldn't use pesticides or strong cleaning agents— affects the way their baby's brain grows.'

'I want her to have a brain,' Emma said dryly.

'That's pretty important to keep in mind, as far as I'm concerned.'

Montana agreed. 'That's what I meant about responsibility. Even a mother's emotions can impact on a baby so if Mum is always sad then the baby thinks it's normal to be feeling sad a lot of the time. That's why I tried not to be too sad when I was pregnant.'

Emma looked up with ready sympathy. 'Why were you sad?'

'I'm a widow. My husband died last year when I was first pregnant and now I have a nearly two-month-old daughter called Dawn. So I am bringing up my daughter without a daddy.'

Montana couldn't help but think of Andy that morning. He'd bounced Dawn on his lap while Montana had been eating and she realised how often she'd come to the kitchen to retrieve her daughter to find Andy chatting away to her as if she understood every word he said.

Dawn thought she had a father. It was an unsettling concept but she needed to concentrate on Emma and think about that curly one later.

Emma was still pondering Montana's loss. 'That is sad. Why did you call her Dawn?'

Montana knew where this was leading and she just hoped it didn't cause too much damage but it was too late now. 'Because she was born right at sunrise.'

Emma nodded. 'In your hospital?'

Montanan smiled wryly. Yep. She'd have to tell her. 'Dawn was born a month early and I was a bit far away at the time. She was born on the side of a mountain.'

'On the side of a mountain?' Emma stared, open-mouthed and horrified. 'Who was with you?'

Montana shrugged. 'Nobody was really with me, although an inquisitive kangaroo and her joey watched me, but Dr Buchanan arrived soon after and my baby and I are both fine.'

Emma shook her head vehemently. 'I am so *not* having my baby on a mountain.' Emma shuddered and her hand crept up to cup her stomach.

Montana needed Emma to know she hadn't planned it. 'I didn't mean that to happen. Dawn just arrived a bit fast.'

Emma's brows drew together ferociously. 'So if you know so much about giving birth, how come you didn't have your baby in a hospital?'

Montana shrugged. 'That's how my birth experience panned out. But that's rare. Usually you have plenty of notice, sometimes days or weeks of warnings, before you go into labour.'

Not quite how she'd choose to explain signs of labour but at least Montana felt she had Emma's attention now. 'Everyone has a different birth, some better or different to others, and we can't really choose which experience we're going to have—we can only learn about choices and the sequence of events to prepare. But we'll talk about that another day because it's a long time before you have to think of your baby's birth.'

'Thank goodness for that.' Emma shuddered. 'I'm gonna have a 'sarean.'

'Caesarean.' Montana suppressed a smile and left that for another time as well.

She moved on. 'So what other symptoms of pregnancy have you had, apart from nausea?'

Emma shrugged. 'I cry a lot but I'll try to think of happier things now because I *do not* want my baby to be sad all the time.'

The vehemence in Emma's voice surprised them both and Montana nodded. 'It's different when you think of your baby as real and needing you to mother it even before it's born, isn't it?'

'How come Tommy gets off so lightly? He doesn't have to worry about anything now until she's born.'

'No.' Montana risked a tease. 'Nothing. Except that your brothers want to kill him!'

Emma shrugged again. 'I'm the one who had to fix that, too,' she said dryly, and Montana laughed.

An hour later Montana heard Dawn cry and she closed the book and stood up. 'That's it for today, Emma. My baby calls. Come and meet Dawn.'

When they moved out to the veranda Andy was there and both women stopped to watch him as he carried Dawn to the edge of the veranda.

CHAPTER FIVE

ANDY had Dawn under his arm like a little pink football and to him she felt incredibly warm and precious tucked into his side as she gazed up at him with her gorgeous wide eyes.

'Mummy is busy at the moment, poppet,' he said. 'She's inside, honest, and you have to come out with me and look at all the trees waving in the breeze.'

She was such a cutie, like her mother, Andy thought as he swung her up into his other arm and turned towards the water. 'See the big black swans? They look like ships on the lake. Maybe you and me and Mummy could go for a trip in a boat one day. You'd like that.'

Dawn gurgled and pursed her lips and cooed as if trying to impart a secret to him and he grinned down at her. 'You're talking. Yes, you are. Such an advanced little thing that you are at only eight weeks. It must be the company. Your Uncle Andy is always here for you. You just give me a yell and I can come and talk to you.'

He heard the door open behind him and turned to see Montana and Emma had finished.

The warm feeling in Montana's stomach threatened to spill over into tears and she couldn't watch any more. 'Are you two having a nice time?' she said as she turned away in case he saw the shininess in her eyes.

She beckoned to Emma. 'Come and meet her, Emma.'

Emma edged across shyly and stroked Dawn's little foot. 'She's so tiny.'

Montana laughed. 'She's big now. Your baby will be even tinier.'

Andy smiled at Emma. 'Hello. Did you have a good morning?'

'You bet.' Emma said, and he could see the difference in her already. He sighed with relief. She clutched a bag of reading material and grinned up at him. Montana had magic all right, but he'd known that.

He watched Montana studying Emma and the glow in his chest came back as if someone had poked at a fire with a stick and blown on it.

He looked away to the girl. 'So when are you coming back, Emma?'

Emma looked at both of them to see if she had it correct. 'This time next week, if that's OK? Montana said she'd talk to my year advisor at school and we'll do a child studies project as we go along. That will help with my marks when I have to leave school in the middle of the year.'

'Great idea. I'll run you home, then.' Andy held out his hand and Montana handed him the car keys.

His hand strayed to her shoulder as she turned away and she stopped. 'Why don't you come with us, Montana? We could drive around the lake on the way home.' He knew he'd enjoy her company—it just depended on her.

His hand dropped but he could still feel her warmth on his fingers. Touching her felt as good as he'd known it would and just as dangerous. 'I've seen Louisa and she said she'll keep lunch for us.'

Montana smiled. 'I'd like that.'

His chest expanded as he stood back to allow her to precede them down the steps. Life was good and today was especially delightful.

After they dropped Emma home Andy drove the scenic route back in the opposite direction around the lake because he enjoyed the tranquillity—and he was in no rush to lose Montana's company.

He took pleasure in everything even more when he was with her. The lake seemed clearer, the sky bluer, even the jagged signs of progress had a certain charm in the distant housing development.

'We haven't been out much since you came, have we?' He had to admit he'd spent a fair bit of time thinking about where he could take her but hadn't actually made it happen yet.

He wondered if she'd even spared him a thought. 'I gather you enjoyed your morning with Emma.'

She turned her face to his and he could see the enthusiasm there he'd hoped Emma would benefit from. 'I did. Yes. She's great.'

She smiled at him and he felt his heart rate pick up just with that attention. Imagine if she did more than smile—he'd be a basket case.

'I hadn't realised how much I missed interacting with pregnant women,' she said. 'Emma's a sweetie.'

You're a sweetie, he thought. 'I'm glad you like her.'

They drove along through fields that sprouted 'For Sale' signs and passed an early development stage of the future housing estate.

'This will be Lakeside Village when it's finished.' They passed thick stands of gumtrees and native shrubs all backdropped by the lake. 'I think it retains the country feel.'

He watched her give the area a three-sixty-degrees and nod. 'The view is great.'

The estate boasted white kerbs and gutters and houseless cul-de-sacs and he found himself thinking for the first time what it would be like to build a house again with a family in mind.

A big house down on his land at the end of the lake with a jetty and a boathouse and a parents' retreat from the hordes of children they'd have.

His daydream halted when he realised that he had a particular mother and child already who would make a great start there. It was lucky she couldn't read his mind or she'd ask him to pull over so she could get out.

'How far away did you say the new mine site is?' Montana was definitely in a different space to him and that was a good thing.

He forced his brain to shelve his future home for later to answer her question. 'Twenty kilometres, but they've put through a straight road and it won't take long to drive between the estate and the mine.'

He frowned. 'That's why I'm hoping the hospital will get the upgrade. We're an hour closer than the base hospital and although the mine does have helicopters which would take the serious casualties away we do want their custom.'

She pondered that. 'When does production start?'

'It's started.' He glanced across at her and then back to the road. Even with that brief look he'd noticed the way her nose had a faint dusting of freckles on the end. Cute.

He frowned at himself and returned to topic. 'They have a tent city at the moment and the company plans to build the first fifty houses at Lakeside in the next six months.'

'That's a big influx of families for a small town. Aren't you happy about that?'

That startled him. 'Why wouldn't I be happy?'

She tilted her head and examined his expression. 'You had a fractious look on your face.'

'Fractious.' He grinned at her observation. At

least he wasn't invisible to her. 'No. I'd be happy. Not just for the town either. It's a godsend for those further out on the land trying to hang onto their properties until the next rain.'

He pondered the stress some of his more distant patients lived under. 'We've quite a contingent from up to two hundred miles west coming in to work at the mine. Those farmers without trades fill positions like mine maintenance or driving trucks. And then there are the extra three hundred skilled workers that will come in when the mine becomes fully productive.'

'Exciting times for Lyrebird Lake,' she said. No doubt she could see his enthusiasm and also, no doubt, he amused her.

He grinned at her observation. 'It is. That spells changes not just to the services like the hospital and schools, but the shopping, and of course the pubs will do a roaring trade.'

She nodded sagely. 'More babies for our new maternity unit.'

'I like the way your mind works.' He chuckled. 'We have to talk about that. Have you thought any more about setting up the caseload birth centre?'

'I am interested if I can get the midwives.'

He sighed with relief and pulled over so he could concentrate on her comments without having to divide his attention.

His relief was out of proportion to the situation. He hadn't realised how much he'd dreaded that she mightn't want to stay. That in itself was a concern for his state of mind. 'Do you think you could attract other midwives here as well?'

She considered her answer. 'With case load? The idea of a midwifery-run clinic? I think there is real appeal there. Nearly every clinic I know has waiting lists of midwives who want to do case load.'

She went on thoughtfully, 'It's the hospitals that have trouble finding staff to work in areas midwives don't want to—under conditions that don't suit them. Case load is so flexible and rewarding if you have a good team.'

He didn't quite get it but he knew it worked well in other areas. 'I understand the concept but the finer points you'll have to explain to me.'

'Sure, but what about you? You won't be able to keep up with just Ned.'

'I know.' He sighed. 'I've put a few feelers out and if I can't get any stayers then I'll just have to pull a few favours and think in short-term appointments until we do find someone.'

He took one hand off the steering-wheel where it rested and gestured to the rolling hills in the distance. 'This place has grown to mean a lot to me and I want to see it work for a lot of reasons.'

'I begin to see why you suggested I come here.'

He turned his head and looked at her. He could feel his lips twitch at the corners. 'Do you?'

He gestured to the grassy verged picnic spot and

turned to face her. 'Do you want to get out and sit at the table for a while? Dawn can lie on the rug and watch the leaves, maybe.'

There he was again. Thinking ahead and including Dawn. How many men would do that as well as Andy did? she thought. 'Sure.'

The conversation faltered while they settled themselves and Dawn to face the lake. The soft breeze was warm but pleasant. Birds swooped and dived into the lake and further out a dinghy with two young boys drifted as they fished.

'All this organising at the hospital.' She watched one of the boys reel in a fish. 'It's a big job to liaise on your own.'

He thought about that and then shook his head. 'I'm not really on my own. The mayor is supportive and happy to mediate with state government for the funding and building upgrades we need.' He ticked them off on his fingers.

'The project officer at the mine is an old school friend and she's promised to push for support from the company for capital works and cheap rent for hospital employees when the houses are built.'

'You've already done a lot, then.'

'I'm stuck a little at the hospital. The current matron is not interested in midwifery and she has enough on her plate with the changes. She's threatened to leave as soon as we find a replacement but she'd hate it if I did because she's not really in a hurry to sever all ties.'

'And you're telling me this because…?'

He grinned again. 'I wondered if you'd be up to that sort of commitment some time in the future?'

Montana shook her head. 'Not in full-time work.'

He wasn't daunted. He could work with that. 'What about three days a week and we'd get you a trainee administrative assistant as well so you could still be hands on in the midwifery clinic when it opens?'

He watched her consider it and his pulse rate picked up again. 'That's more attractive,' she said slowly. 'What about Dawn?'

Hell, he'd arrange what ever she wanted. 'We're still a country hospital. Louisa is there but we could set up a nursery in your office if you wanted or on the ward and even find a young woman to help you as a nanny-cum-receptionist.'

Montana looked at him as he demolished problems with a one-track mind. His green eyes blazed with determination to build up the hospital services and she could only admire his tenacity, but he was pushing her.

She had other things to think about. 'You've put a lot of thought into this.'

'I'll admit I hoped you might be interested. I think you could bring a lot to the hospital and the town.'

Her brow crinkled. 'I don't understand why you have such faith in me.' She didn't think that any-body had ever seen such potential as Andy had decided she had. It was an odd feeling and one that left her strangely warmed at his confidence, but it was not something she was accustomed to.

He shrugged. 'I do have faith in you. Plus our current matron, Joan, is not enjoying the administrative tasks that are mounting up and she'd flip if I mentioned the birth centre as well. The hospital needs someone who would relish that challenge.'

Would she relish the challenge? In all honesty, probably, yes. 'And you think I'm that person?'

She watched his face and there was no doubt there. How did he really see her?

He said, 'I would highly recommend you to the board without a qualm.'

What if she let him down? Moved on? 'You've never asked about my other qualifications.'

'Westside Admin told me you were in charge of their unit at Westside and instrumental in setting up the free-standing centre there. Misty said you were very good at managing people. I saw that in the week at your house.' He grinned. 'I know you've got the paperwork and the experience.'

Montana gazed out over the lake and she could feel the ties binding her to a place she wasn't sure she wanted to be bound to for reasons that were way too complicated to think about now.

She had become even more suspicious of her feelings for Andy let alone if she committed to the exposure of working with him at the hospital.

What about Douglas and Douglas's house in

town and all her things? What about her old friends and her old life?

And the last, startling, dreadful thought—Douglas hadn't even been gone a year!

What disloyalty was this?

She couldn't help loving it here. Douglas would never have assumed she could do all the things Andy believed she could.

She shied away from that because it involved negative thoughts of Douglas and comparisons. The next thing she'd be thinking she could hope and dream for things in the future.

'It's a big commitment. To tell the truth, part of the attraction here is the lack of commitment required. I'd have to change the way I picture the future. I'd have to think about it seriously and not rush into anything.'

Andy was nodding, but there was that glint of determination in his eye that she was becoming more wary of. 'Fine. Believe me, time's not a problem.'

Why did she not accept what he said as true? she thought with a smile. He was one-eyed and too passionate about looking after his town, that's why.

He scooped up Dawn, who had suddenly decided she didn't want to lie on her stomach any more, and went on blithely with her tucked under his arm.

'How about in the morning we take a trip up to the hospital and chat to Joan? She could give you an idea of what's involved in the deputy's job and then you could see how you feel about the idea.'

She knew it. She picked up the blanket and shook it in preparation to leave. 'That's rushing.'

'Nah.' He flapped his hand and shifted Dawn onto his hip. Her little fists waved around joyfully. 'The next board meeting is five days away.'

'Gee, thanks. A whole five days to think about it.' But she couldn't help smiling at his single-mindedness.

The next morning they left Dawn with Louisa again.

Montana couldn't help a stab of guilt when her daughter cried as they drove off to the hospital. This must be how all working mothers felt as they drove away but it didn't help the burden of remorse she seemed to be accumulating. Then again Dawn could be crying that Andy had left.

'She'll be fine. You know it,' Andy consoled her, but knowing Dawn enjoyed being with Louisa didn't help.

'Maybe it's not time to go back to work yet.' Montana chewed her lip.

'Maybe not.' Andy understood and that helped. 'We'll see what you think after this morning. But you know that Dawn will be fine with Louisa.'

The administration offices were in the original stone part of the building with wooden window-frames that pulled straight up so you lean out over the gardens if you wanted to.

The building had high ceilings and an old fireplace in the boardroom. It resembled the beer garden at the back of an old pub with wooden-backed chairs around the big oak table that dominated the room.

Matron's office was tucked away to the side of the boardroom, next to an empty office, and jam-packed with old medical books, black ledgers and a towering filing cabinet that looked older than the woman who waited for them with a frail out-stretched hand.

Joan Winterbourne was nudging seventy but the snow-white bun caught tightly on her head pulled the wrinkled folds of her face up nicely so that she looked vaguely oriental in appearance and ten years younger than her age.

'So you've managed to get her here finally, Andy,' she said as she took Montana's hand and pumped it. 'Welcome, welcome to my nightmare.'

Andy grinned. 'It's not that bad, Joan. You'll scare Montana off with your negativity.'

'Pshaw,' Joan scoffed. 'Young people aren't scared of anything these days. Especially a challenge. If I was twenty years younger I'd take it on myself but I find changes and bureaucrats exhausting. Still, it's my fault. I won't learn to e-mail and the fax is broken.'

Andy shook his head. 'You should have told me your fax was broken. I'll have a new one here this afternoon.'

'You don't need to be running after me, as well as everyone else, Andy,' she said, but Montana could tell Joan was touched by Andy's care.

'You know I don't mind.' Andy changed the subject. 'I thought I'd show Montana what a great little hospital we have with a quick tour. Do you want to come?'

'Sounds good, but I'm expecting a call so I'll pass. But you have fun.'

Joan waved them off and they left by a side door to cross the garden and enter into the larger building.

'So you mentioned to Joan a while ago I might be interested in helping her?' Montana slanted a look at him as he walked beside her to the next building.

He didn't meet her eyes. 'I could have done.'

'Cagey, aren't you?' She stopped and waited for him to stop, too, then narrowed her eyes at him. 'When?'

He smiled. 'About a month ago. I was waiting for you to get bored.'

'What faith you have in me, sir.'

'I do, don't I?' She wondered why that comment of his hit a hollow nerve under her rib cage but decided it was probably a need for coffee. Things had been a little hectic that morning and she'd missed out.

They entered by the side door of the emergency department. The area housed an observation ward, two triage bays and a minor operating theatre. The office looked over the half a dozen plastic chairs in the waiting room, two of which were occupied.

Andy gestured with his arm. 'We have facilities

to keep three patients in beds here and two in the triage bays if we have to.'

A nurse was undressing a familiar looking man's bandaged arm and Andy paused beside her to check the healing process on the patient.

'You remember Paul, from the flying club? He burnt his arm last Friday at another barbecue and Chrissie's been dressing it every day. Chrissie is our registered nurse on duty. Chrissie, this is Montana— she's the midwife staying with Ned and I.'

Paul waved his unbandaged hand. 'You'll have to wait for me to heal before I can take you up,' he said, and Montana nodded sagely.

Chrissie smiled. 'Hi, there, Montana. I hear you made quite a hit with Emma yesterday.'

Montana smiled at the tall blonde woman. 'Word gets around.'

'Not much misses the bush telegraph around here.' Chrissie put her hand to her ear and pretended to listen. Her hand dropped and she grinned. 'Actually, her father is my cousin.'

Montana smiled back. 'I'll remember that.'

Andy nodded at Paul's arm. 'It's looking a lot better, Paul. I reckon your wife could bandage that now. Just come back Monday for a final check or sooner if you have any worries. OK?'

'Thanks, Andy. I'll drop a turkey off for Louisa. We're culling at home and she said she'd like one for Ned's party.'

'Thanks. Just don't get germs in your burn,

mate.' Andy grinned and tapped him on the back before he turned to Chrissie.

'Anybody you worried about in the waiting room, Chrissie?'

She shook her head. 'Not at the moment. Just two for dressings. And Bill said Eva's observations are fine so we'll continue with your plans to send her home after four hours. The base hospital rang and confirmed the X-ray shows no skull fractures. She wasn't unconscious for more than a few seconds.'

A male nurse filled out a patient chart at the end of the only occupied bed. Andy crossed to him and Montana followed.

'Bill is our enrolled nurse who doubles as an orderly when we need things moved. He's a jack of all trades and we'd be lost without him.'

Bill, a short, thin man who could have been a jockey, held out his hand and shook Montana's. 'Andy's just saying that because he wants me to take all the oxygen cylinders into town and get them exchanged. And pick up doughnuts.'

He gestured to the patient and lowered his voice. 'Eva's asleep but she's easily woken.'

Andy nodded and checked the chart before they moved on to tour the main ward.

The ward area was divided into five female and five male beds—three with elderly patients in them—and two ancillary rooms plus a staff cafeteria just off the kitchen.

'The enrolled nurses run this end and the RN on

duty comes through from Outpatients and give any S8 medications when needed. Otherwise the nurses down here are self-sufficient. So what do you think?'

Andy was like a proud father and she thought it endearing he could be so proud of a hospital. She still thought he needed a life, though.

'Your baby is very nice. Now—where would the midwifery happen?'

He raised his eyebrows suggestively. 'Nitty-gritty, eh?' He spun on his heel and gestured for her to follow him.

'There's a wing tacked onto the main building. Come and I'll show you. It was offered to me as accommodation but I much preferred to stay with Ned and Louisa.'

He spoke over his shoulder. 'I thought about offering it to you but I'm glad I didn't. I'd have missed out on Dawn and I'm very fond of her.' He paused as if he was going to add something else but didn't.

There was a twinkle in his eye and she wondered what else he'd been thinking, but then they arrived and Andy found a key on his keyring that opened the door.

'The wing has a couple of big rooms and a heap of small ones and is self-contained,' he said.

The hallway was dusty and the room needed airing but when Montana pulled up the blinds sunlight flooded in through windows and she could see the outlook was splendid.

The wing even had a walled courtyard that clients could use in labour and still have privacy.

Andy stood in the hallway and watched her indulgently, amused when she muttered under her breath and generally just enjoyed her reactions.

Montana pushed open doors and pulled blinds and when she'd finished she turned to face him with a smile that made him feel like he'd just seen a sunburst.

'It could be perfect. It's a great building. Not too big and not too small.'

Her excitement transmitted easily to him. 'There's nothing structural that needs doing and we even have a big bath.'

He could feel himself frown and tried to erase it. He wasn't sure he was comfortable with water births as such. 'Why do you want a bath?'

'Pain relief,' she said sweetly, and changed the subject. 'We could caseload easily here and open it only when someone was in labour. That way you wouldn't have staff on duty when they weren't needed and if you had three or four midwives on a roster, there would be no problem manning it for the amount of births we'd start off with.'

Andy loved to see her so enthusiastic and motivated. It reminded him of himself when he talked about the hospital but he still had that little concern about the bath. But he'd follow up on that later when she'd settled down.

'I've been onto the base hospital,' he said. 'They

have leftover equipment from refurbishing if you want to think about a shopping list, and we have some funding from the ladies' hospital auxiliary.

'We'd have to talk to Carrie, our auxiliary president, but if you produce a proposal that covers most things, I'd be happy to support you to the board and the auxiliary for purchases.'

Montana spun slowly around again, assessing the rooms. 'It could all happen fairly quickly— the physical part, that is. The government requirements, staffing and the liaison with the base for emergencies would take longer. Say four or five months.'

'Well in time for Emma,' Andy suggested, and they both smiled.

He watched her face and realised he hadn't felt so positive for along time. 'I was thinking maybe before then you could move your well-women's clinic over here and maybe even antenatal classes.'

She twirled and extended her arms. 'I love the way you think. I'm very excited, Andy.'

He could tell. Her eyes shone and she looked as if she'd like to grab him and kiss him. He wished.

But that wasn't why he'd brought her here, and he needed to remember that. He'd brought her here to establish this service and broaden the staff skill mix. 'I'm pretty keen myself.'

Back at the doctors' residence that evening Montana slipped out of her room after settling Dawn to sleep. The house was encircled by wide verandas and Montana's room was positioned a few doors along the high-ceilinged central hallway from Andy's.

Despite the close proximity of all their sleeping arrangements, she'd never heard any noises from other parts of the house when the doors were shut or actually even seen the door open to Andy's room.

Unusually, today Andy's door stood open, and she couldn't help but glance in as she passed.

She blinked and looked again. Andy stood in the centre of a huge wood-panelled room dressed only in jockey shorts. Acres of strong brown chest seemed to fill Montana's vision and after another quick stunned look Montana swung her head away and quickened her step.

Andy's voice followed her. 'Stop! Montana, wait.' Montana turned back towards him with her gaze firmly anchored on the high ceiling.

Andy chuckled. 'Come on, Sister Brown, I'm sorry I shocked you, but you've seen guys in their jocks before.'

Montana rolled her eyes. 'Come on Andy. How about if I stand with my door open in my bra and undies and call out to you as you go past. Please.'

Andy grinned hugely. 'Now, that's an idea. Any time.'

'Men!' She resumed her progress down the hall and he came out in all his glory to call after her.

'Wait, Montana. Can I have your help for a second, please? Really.'

He lowered his voice. 'We're having a surprise birthday for Ned's seventieth and I'd like to buy a kilt and jacket on the internet. I have to give measurements and I've always been hopeless at estimating clothes sizes.'

Andy stood there, six feet plus of gloriously muscled male swinging a tape measure in skin-tight black cotton underwear that left nothing to the imagination.

Suddenly there wasn't enough air in the hallway, maybe not enough in the whole of Lyrebird Lake, and she could feel the heat creep up her neck.

Looking at someone couldn't make you faint so she must be coming down with something. Her tongue felt dry against the roof of her mouth and she looked down at her clenched hands. She moistened her lips and forced herself to answer past her dry throat.

She coughed. She was definitely coming down with something. 'A kilt and jacket would need to fit well. The hardest thing would be the jacket.' She glanced again at Andy and the last bit came out in a squeak.

Andy didn't seem to notice. 'I could overcome that if you help me. Ned's been at me to buy a kilt because my ancestors were Scots, too, and I want to surprise him on the night.'

'Clan Buchanan?' She raised her eyebrows in disbelief.

'Of Buchanan Castle. I looked it up on the internet.'

'OK. I'll suspend belief. Don't you want to go to a shop and get fitted? That's what most people do.'

'No way to do that here and I don't have the time to go elsewhere. Please. I could really do with some help.'

He held up a printed sheet on a clipboard. 'I've typed them all on here.'

Montana chewed her lip and pictured herself running the tape measure intimately over Andy. The picture was a little too graphic and she blushed again and avoided his eyes.

Silly, but she couldn't help this swamped feeling that had come out of nowhere. 'There must be a seamstress in town who'd be better at this than me.'

Despite the almost overwhelming impulse to do just that, she looked anywhere but at him. 'Or what about Louisa?'

'The local seamstress would let everyone know what I'm doing and I want it to be a surprise. And I want to surprise Louisa, too.'

She didn't think she could do this.

CHAPTER SIX

RELUCTANTLY Montana accepted the tape measure and sucked in her breath. She avoided his eyes— she could do this.

Andy would be embarrassed too, she reassured herself, but when she looked at him again to check the validity of that thought, he winked at her like a mischievous six-year-old.

The emotion that shone out of those wicked green eyes was not embarrassment. It was pure unholy amusement.

She looked away hurriedly and ran her fingers over the thin white tape as she psyched herself up for something she definitely wasn't comfortable with.

He wasn't going to go away. And she wasn't going to let him know how hard this would be. So, she let her breath out and moved closer.

Her words came out quietly as she compressed her lips. 'Let's get it over with then.'

Andy stood tall, lifted his chin, and spoke to the

top of her head. 'That was brusque. I wouldn't like you to be too thrilled at the prospect of measuring my manly stature.'

'I'll try not to be.' She lifted his arm and he let it flop down again without taking the weight. His shoulders shook and she could feel a tiny giggle inside that she refused to allow to escape.

'Hold up your arm, please.' She rolled her eyes. 'Arm length,' she intoned and then measured inside and outlengths, ignoring the subtle firmness of the muscles under her fingers. 'I'll measure and you write it down.'

He rested the clipboard on top of the old-fashioned table so she could see what was needed and did what he was told between measurements. Biddable at present, she noted suspiciously.

'Wrist.' She measured and waited for Andy to write it down.

The next request made her stomach flicker and then she swallowed. 'Biceps.'

His shoulders shook again and she closed her eyes. She'd known it would get harder.

'Do you want it flexed or deflexed?' he said.

She slanted a look at him but his head was too high to see his expression. 'You're enjoying this.'

He looked down and grinned. 'I'm having a ball.'

She chewed her lip again and thought about biceps. 'I don't know. Flexed I guess.'

Andy obliged and the tape measure trembled.

Montana changed her mind. 'Um, deflexed, I think. Otherwise the fabric will be too…' Her voice trailed off and he grinned again.

This was too much and he was not making it any easier. Her temper slipped a little. 'For goodness' sake, Andy. Get over yourself.'

His chest trembled with suppressed laughter. 'Come on, Montana. This is hilarious.'

Despite herself she giggled. 'OK. I'll try not to stress.' She had trouble concentrating. 'Chest maybe?'

Andy shook his head as if she were a slow child. 'Just follow the prompts on the sheet. We need a shoulder width first.'

She glared at him. 'How about you read it and I'll measure where you tell me?'

His eyebrows shot up wickedly. 'That could be fun.'

She looked at the tape in her hand. 'Stop teasing me or I'm out of here.'

He pulled his twitching smile into a serious face and lowered his voice until it was very deep. 'Please, measure the shoulder width.'

She did. 'Done.'

'Neck.'

'Can I pull it tight?' Her voice was sweet even if her intent was not.

He loosened it from around his neck. 'Be nice. Now the chest.' The tape measure pulled tightly when he breathed in and she was secretly impressed.

That new hollow in her chest seemed to glow as if someone had turned on a light in there.

'Done,' she mumbled less clearly.

'Waist,' he said, and the laughter was back in his voice.

She steeled herself to circle his hips with the tape measure and slide it up to his waist. The feel of his skin inside her wrists and forearms left more glowing warmth she ached to rub away but she didn't want to draw attention to it. 'Done.' Her voice squeaked a little.

'From armpit to waist and armpit to hip.' That was easier. She could do that.

'Inner thigh,' he said in a bored voice.

Montana checked his face for humour but even though she couldn't see him laughing she suspected he was beside himself. 'Do your own.'

He exaggerated the measurement. 'That would be enormous,' he said.

'Like your head. Give it to me. I'm a nurse. I can do this.' She measured. 'Done.'

'Outside waist to knee.' It was a long way and she had to get down on the floor to measure. His legs seemed to stretch for ever from his waist.

'Inner thigh to knee.'

'It does not ask for that.' She snatched the sheet to check and there it was. Andy laughed.

'I don't believe this. You made up these measurements. You are some sicko voyeur. It's a skirt, for heaven's sake.'

'Kilt,' he corrected. 'That's the last one. You want me to move the tackle out of the way?'

'I think you could manage that one and the tackle.' No way was she going near there. 'Thank goodness for that. I was working up a sweat.'

'And a very nice glow it was. I only added a few when I typed it up.'

She'd kill him. And then she looked up at him.

The mood in the room changed subtly, although it was still fun and she really couldn't remember when she'd felt this bubbly. She wasn't sure how it had happened but she'd become too serious over the last few years since she'd married Douglas.

In fact, she couldn't remember ever doing something as mad and, now she looked back on it, as screamingly funny as measuring Andy. Douglas had taken himself a little too seriously to ever have trusted Montana to measure up a tailored outfit for him.

Just to look at Andy made her smile. They were standing close together and she could feel the warmth emanating from him—or maybe it was coming from her, because she certainly felt heated.

He leant down and brushed her cheek with his lips. 'Thanks, Montana. I really appreciated that.' He added very softly, 'Best fun I've had all year.'

She wasn't sure if he meant the measuring or the kiss, but she felt strangely removed from the world and fuzzy, and when he kissed her forehead she tilted her face toward his.

His eyes seemed to be all she could see until she

noticed his mouth. It looked soft and curved and delightful… He lowered his head and of course their lips met.

Just a fleeting, impersonal kiss. Or was it?

No, not impersonal. This was the first, brief, gentle touch of magic and the first breath of a new life, the first man in her space since Douglas, and while it was different from all that had gone before, it felt mystically right and wonderful.

Too wonderful. On her side anyway.

He stepped back and neither of them said anything. There was no need to talk or to take it further at this moment. But she'd certainly have to think about this later.

His mobile beeped softly and he moved away to listen and yet his eyes stayed on hers.

He terminated the call and slipped the phone back into his pocket. All the laughter was gone from his eyes.

'Do you want to come with me while I visit Emma's mother? She's had another fall.'

'Sure.' Montana's response was quick but it took a few seconds more for her brain to clear as she followed him. She'd think about that other moment later. 'If you don't think I'll be in the way.'

He'd thrown on clothes over his jocks while she'd still been dazed and now he stood at the door with his car keys in his hand.

'I can introduce you and say we were coming to meet them anyway. Come on.'

* * *

Emma's parents lived opposite the lake in a rambling old farmhouse with wide verandas. The garden in the front yard was full of roses and they passed under a bloom-laden arch spanning the path and bush after bush of colour amongst lush greenery and rocks.

'How beautiful. I love roses.' She turned to Andy, who was following, and he smiled at her pleasure.

'I must get you a Blue Moon. Palest lavender blue rose. Clare has them round the back.'

It seemed a strange thing to say, she thought. 'Why that one?'

'I saw a web page on rose meanings once,' he said cryptically, then changed the subject. 'Clare is an avid gardener, though she says even that isn't giving her pleasure at the moment.'

He frowned as he thought about his patient.

Emma opened the door at his knock and Montana noted how the young girl's stomach showed roundness more noticeably now. Emma blinked when she saw Montana.

Andy loomed behind her. 'Hi, Emma. Montana and I were together when you called. I hope you don't mind that I brought her.'

Emma shook her head. 'Of course not. Come in, both of you. Mum's in the lounge. She's still cross I called you.'

Andy patted her shoulder. 'You did the right thing. What happened?'

Emma brushed her hair out of her eyes. 'She was tying trellis in the back yard and she got tangled up in the ladder when she was coming down. She's getting worse. Her balance is off and she's so clumsy. Now I think she's got a twitch.'

Montana could see that Emma instinctively knew there was something seriously not right with her mother and Andy frowned at Emma's description as if something had triggered a thought.

He led the way to the lounge, where Clare was busy dusting the mantelpiece. As they came into the room a photo frame went flying off the mantelpiece and landed on the floor, where it cracked in two on the floor.

Clare said, 'Blast!'

Emma looked at Andy and Montana as if to say, *See!*

Andy paused and studied Clare for a moment and Montana saw the instant when the diagnosis suggested itself to him.

He stiffened and then his shoulders slumped slightly before he pulled himself together.

He turned and met Montana's eyes and the shock she saw there made her draw a quick breath.

'What's wrong?' Emma was no slouch and she knew something significant had happened.

Emma crossed to Andy and tugged at his sleeve. 'What is it? What's wrong with her?'

Clare turned and saw them and Montana could see the tears in her eyes. 'Oh. Hello. Excuse me.'

She picked up the broken frame. 'I hate this. I was never an uncoordinated person.'

She saw Montana and tried to smile. Andy repeated what he'd said to Emma about them being together. 'And I wanted to introduce you Montana as she's helping Emma with her antenatal information.'

'Yes. I think Emma said something about that.' Clare made a visible effort to remember and held out her hand. Her fingers twitched a little as she put her hand in Montana's and smiled perfunctorily. 'It's nice to meet you.'

Then Clare dropped Montana's hand as if she'd forgotten she held it and reached up to brush the tears from her face before she turned to Andy. 'Andy? What happening to me.'

Andy patted Emma's hand and moved across to her mother. He put his arm around Clare and drew her back to the lounge. 'Please, sit down, Clare.'

He quickly checked her over from her fall and then pulled a little torch from his pocket to check her pupils. 'Are you sore anywhere from your fall?'

'No, I'm fine.' She frowned at her daughter and then turned back to him. 'Emma shouldn't have bothered you.'

'I'm glad she did. She did the right thing.' He sighed as he watched her perch anxiously on the edge of the lounge and then he crouched down beside her. 'I'm not sure, Clare, but I'd like to get you tested for an inherited neurological disease called Huntington's.'

Montana's breath sucked in silently as she saw where Andy was coming from. It was a bold diagnosis with little evidence but she didn't doubt Andy's perception. Montana felt her heart squeeze for the journey ahead for Clare if what Andy said was true. And also for Emma.

He waited for a response but Clare didn't react so he pushed on. 'At first I thought your symptoms might have been from the car accident but they aren't following the pattern I expected. Your fingers seem a little shakier today and there are some diseases that cause symptoms like yours. This particular one I'm thinking of can do that but it doesn't make sense yet.'

Clare looked up at him and compressed her lips to stop them trembling. 'I will get better though, won't I?'

'I'd need to do a blood test to know these things. There is always a family history of Huntington's and usually people have an idea they are at risk of it. Are your parents alive, Clare?'

Clare shook her head. 'They died in a car accident in their early thirties.'

'And their parents?'

'I'm not sure how they died.'

'OK. We'll run some tests. Are you finding tasks more difficult? Do things you could normally do seem trickier now?'

Clare raised her eyes to his and nodded. 'Even getting dressed in the morning seems to take for ever with these clumsy fingers.'

Andy rubbed the back of his neck. 'I'll chat to someone in Brisbane and we'll get some blood sent away for genetic testing. But in the meantime it might be better if you didn't drive the car.'

'Genetic testing?' Clare heard that bit and the alarm in her eyes caused Andy to reach down and grip her hands in both of his in support for a minute. Montana could see that Andy shared his patient's distress.

Clare went on slowly, as if she dreaded to say the words, 'So if I have this disease then my kids could have it?' She looked at Emma. 'And Emma's baby, too?'

Emma gasped and her hand slid protectively over her stomach. Montana slipped her arm around the young woman and squeezed her shoulders, suddenly glad she had come.

Andy gripped Clare's hand once more and then sat back a little to look into her face. He held up his hands. 'I'm nowhere near sure that's what it is but we will find out. Let's not panic and get ahead of ourselves.'

Andy met Clare's eyes and spoke quietly but firmly. 'You will both have lots of questions and I'll make sure I can answer all of them.'

He turned to Emma. 'Try and remember that even if your mother proves positive for this inherited disease, there is the fifty per cent chance of it not being passed down to you and therefore not to your baby.'

To Clare he said, 'Rest and remember the more relaxed you are the less the symptoms will be noticeable. Stress is going to make most medical conditions worse. I'll come back later and take some blood and I'll have a chat to my friend in Brisbane as well before I return.'

'I think I'll lie down,' Clare said, and she shook her head at Emma when she moved to help her. 'I'll be right by myself. Show Andy and his friend out, please, Emma.'

They said their goodbyes and as they drove away Montana could still see the alarm in Emma's eyes as she watched them go.

Montana examined Andy's profile and she ached for his silent distress. 'You do think it is Huntington's disease, don't you?'

Andy flicked a glance at her and then he sighed heavily as if he found it difficult to show Montana even a little of what was churning him up inside. 'I'm pretty sure.'

He sighed again. 'It all makes sense. The progression has been slow but the symptoms are there when you look, and it all slots into place.'

He shook his head as if disgusted with himself for taking so long to think of that answer.

'She's had short-term memory loss, fidgeting, depression and apathy, which is so unlike Clare. Now that she has the involuntary movements in her fingers and toes, everything ties in.'

Montana puckered her forehead and then shook

her head. 'I think you are being too hard on yourself. It's still pretty tenuous. I'd never have thought of Huntington's. It's not your everyday disease. And how could she not know about a family disease like that?' The link wasn't there, that Montana could see. 'Without the family history, Huntington's doesn't even come up.'

Andy rubbed the back of his neck again as if it ached. 'I think you'll find there will be an aunt or uncle or grandparent somewhere in the past who didn't die young. Obviously one of her parents had the gene but died in the car accident before they were diagnosed.'

'So it can't skip a generation?' Montana asked, and she shivered at Clare's prognosis.

'You're thinking of Emma and her baby? And Emma's brothers.'

She nodded. 'It's a terrible thing to have hanging over your head.'

Andy watched the road intently and she had no doubt his brain was racing. 'This disease usually doesn't manifest until the person is in their thirties or forties. It can even be as late as a person's seventies and in that case the disease is often mild.'

Best-case scenario. 'So they could get it late and mild if they were lucky.'

Andy slapped the steering-wheel at the unfairness and Montana thought again how much she admired his empathy for his patients. 'Lucky? Yeah.' he said.

They both fell silent and then he added, 'I guess we have to think about some unfortunate people who have juvenile onset—but thankfully that's rare.'

Montana didn't know how to comfort Andy. 'Can you treat Clare if this is what her problem is?'

He glanced across at her briefly and his face reflected his sombre thoughts. 'Only supportively. But I will do everything I can for her and her family. We'll make sure they have the support they need but if Clare has inherited the gene then it's activated and her central nervous system is breaking down. Her symptoms are only going to get worse and eventually she'll require full-time professional care.'

Montana stared at the road in front, too, and she could feel the shock course through her. 'That's horrific.'

Andy sighed heavily. 'The disease has a fairly slow progress and Clare could live another twenty years, a few of those fairly normally.'

'How few?' Montana was thinking how hard this must be for Andy as a friend of the family.

He took one hand off the steering-wheel to rub his neck again and Montana wanted to slide her hand across his shoulders and gently soothe him herself.

'Clare will have enough warning to modify her lifestyle so she can stay at home for as long as possible, but each year will be harder. We can all only pray someone finds a cure before then,' Andy said quietly.

The mood in the car was low and Montana thought again of Emma and her baby. 'Is there much hope for a cure?'

Andy turned and met her eyes briefly. 'There's always hope.'

'So would you test Emma and her brothers?' She hoped he'd be spared the emotions of actual testing and diagnosis.

'We'd better make sure that's what it is first, but I'd suggest it, though the choice is up to them. It's not something they should rush into.'

He sighed. 'Actually, I'd prefer to refer them to Brisbane for proper genetic counselling before the predictive test. I'd hate to let them down by wrong information or not enough right information.'

Montana thought about it. 'I imagine some people would choose not to be tested until they are in their thirties so they can enjoy their life without knowing what's ahead.'

He nodded. 'The "lets worry about it if it happens," option, which has some positives going for it. Like Clare's parents. Other people feel they need to plan if they test positive. Either way would colour your life, I imagine.'

They pulled up at the house and Montana put her hand on his arm until he turned towards her.

She weighed her words as if she had just realised a sudden truth. 'It puts living life to the full into perspective, doesn't it?'

There was a pause and then Andy said, 'For me it does.'

He looked at Montana soberly and they both pondered his heartfelt response.

CHAPTER SEVEN

LATER that evening, Andy found Montana out on the veranda leaning against the rail.

Dark clouds obscured the moon and lightning reflected off the lake. A cool breeze brushed the wisps of dark hair back off her face.

'Melancholy miss,' he said, and came to stand beside her.

She looked across at him. 'That's a good description of how I'm feeling.' She bit her lip. 'I can't help thinking about Emma and what she has to go through with her mother, let alone the possibilities to herself.'

He slipped his arm around her shoulders and she could feel the comfort of his caring seep into her like a warm blanket of peace. She just hoped some comfort was going his way too because a lot of what she was feeling was because Andy was hurting so badly.

Then he said, 'Life can be hard but we can only deal with what we are given. The amazing strength

I see in patients and their families during hard times is why I love doing what I do.'

He squeezed her shoulder and dropped his voice and she could hear his sincerity. 'It makes me humble.'

She rubbed the strong fingers that lay across her collarbone. To hear him talk about being humble made her want to throw her arms around him and pull his head down on her chest. His personal pain for Clare and Emma and all their family made her own heart ache.

He would have known them since he'd come here and had only recently helped Emma's family come to terms with Emma's pregnancy crisis. Now another more deadly and terrible crisis was affecting them.

But he was right and the world suddenly seemed a little less incomprehensible.

'Thank you,' she said quietly. 'You put that beautifully, Andy. I do understand. I've had patients who have awed me with their tenacity during a really hard labour and you feel so proud to have had a small part in their journey.'

He squeezed her shoulders one more time and then dropped his arm to lean on the rail beside her and gaze out over the lake. 'Who knows? You and I might have swapped a few more years with our loved ones for the risk of deterioration later in life—or maybe not. No one can tell how we'd react.'

She tried to recall the way Douglas had looked when one of his patients had had to endure hardship, but she couldn't. It hadn't been a big part of his make-up but that was no excuse for not to be able to remember. All she could see was Andy, hurting for Emma's family, and how much she wanted to comfort him.

She tried harder to picture her late husband's face but nothing came. 'I'm having trouble remembering Douglas's face.' The thought horrified her.

Andy looked down at her and brushed her cheek with his finger. 'Don't beat yourself up. It's tough when that starts to happen. I watched a movie once when someone said it helps if you remember a special moment in time rather than just their face. That works for me when I want to remember my wife.'

'Thank you. I'll try that.' It was odd how she could talk about Douglas with Andy but strangely didn't feel as comfortable for him to talk about his wife. In fact she'd rather he didn't and she didn't know why.

In April, Montana started work as the new deputy nurse manager at the hospital. Her tenure was made up of two short administrative days per week to organise the new caseload midwifery unit and two eight-hour clinical days as the registered nurse on duty for the hospital.

On her first morning as a nurse she worked with

Chrissie, who welcomed her with no small degree of excitement and lots of practical help.

Chrissie was superwoman as far as Montana was concerned.

'So you work full time and your husband is away three or four nights a week.' She shook her head at Chrissie. 'How do you manage?'

Chrissie laughed. 'My mum gets my son off to school and my husband helps on weekends, but it's all worth it.'

Montana thought she made it sound a bit easier than it was. 'What's he do?'

'He's a truck whisperer.'

'A what? Never heard of it.'

Chrissie smiled reminiscently. 'That's what he told me when we met. He's really a diesel mechanic but he told me that trucks have emotional problems, just like horses.'

She laughed. 'He's Irish and has kissed the Blarney stone but I love him. When other mechanics can't find the fault, he's the one who goes in and sorts it out. His reputation is spreading faster than he can keep up.'

Montana smiled at the mental picture of an Irishman talking to a tractor about its emotional problems. 'With a man like that, it must be hard when he's away, though.'

Chrissie shrugged. 'We're saving up for a farm and then he'll be able to stay home and work from there. Maybe we'll even have more kids.'

Andy's unmistakable step in the corridor

heralded his arrival. 'What's this about you having kids, Chrissie?'

'Not yet I'm not and you'll be the last to know.' Chrissie looked him up and down. 'You back again, Andy?'

Surprisingly, Andy had dropped in three times before eight in the morning for reasons Montana assumed she'd work out later.

She saw the twinkle in Chrissie's eye as she watched each of Andy's new explanations float past but she didn't get the joke.

Between the occasional outpatient who appeared for dressings or injections, Chrissie had turned out drawers and cupboards so that Montana knew where to find supplies when needed.

'How are you going, Montana?' Andy asked as he skimmed an outpatient chart.

'It's all pretty simple really,' Montana said as she checked expiry dates on medications and restocked dressing packs.

Chrissie bubbled. 'Apart from the occasional disaster, where we do the best we can with what we have, the rest is more like a clinic than an emergency department.

'Speaking of clinics, how come yours is finished over at the house, Andy?' Chrissie had her hands on her hips and Montana laughed.

'It's not. I just came over for some more X-ray forms. I'll see you later,' he said, and sauntered off again.

Chrissie put another empty box in the bin. 'The man's mad but a sweetie. And I have to thank him because having you here is so great. Even if you work part time I'll have more flexibility with my shifts, which will thrill my family.'

She opened another box. 'Imagine if more new staff came! Just having one more midwife on the books helps so much. Poor Rhonda has been out of it for too long and she's over having to be responsible for new babies if one drops in.'

Montana couldn't imagine ever being over midwifery. 'Has Andy told you about the new birthing centre plans?'

Chrissie nodded enthusiastically. 'He mentioned a little and it sounds great. Especially when I think about having another baby myself. Imagine if I didn't have to go away and wait for labour. Imagine if I could have the same person care for me the whole way through.'

'That's how case load works and we want to drum up business. I think you should spread the word,' Montana teased. 'Andy's sister is a midwife. I'm nagging her to pay a visit so I can talk to her about relocating to the Lake.'

Chrissie stopped what she was doing and leant against the bench to study Montana's face. 'Have you known Andy for a long time?' she asked casually.

Montana kept stocking boxes and missed the intensity of Chrissie's gaze. 'No. I've worked with

Misty for the last six years and she's one of my best friends but never caught up with Andy. I met Andy after my baby was born and he suggested I come here to recuperate.'

'Hmm.' Chrissie's comment was non committed. 'He never loses an opportunity for new staff. I guess the Lake is a peaceful place.'

As she finished her sentence the wail of an approaching siren drifted in the window and they looked at each other and smiled. 'Spoke too soon,' Montana said.

'That'll bring Andy back again and it's not even nine o'clock yet,' Chrissie said with a smile.

Montana shut the cupboard she'd been arranging and moved towards the emergency bay. 'You see a lot of him over here, don't you?'

'Some days more than others,' Chrissie said cryptically, and came to stand beside her as they waited.

The siren turned out to be a police car carrying Chrissie's eight-year-old son, Dylan, who had fallen off his bike on the way to school.

His left arm was swollen at the wrist and he began to cry in earnest when he saw his mother.

The policeman, Bob, and his wife, June, had scooped him from the road and June had him on her lap while her husband drove. June was almost as upset as Dylan.

Chrissie and Montana lifted him carefully and carried him into the observation room.

By the time Andy arrived, Chrissie had consoled Dylan and arranged for the retired technician to come in and X-ray her son's arm and Montana had plied Bob and June with tea for their nerves.

An hour later the results were through and Andy was happy to manage Dylan conservatively. 'Even though his radius and ulna are cracked, the base hospital has confirmed it won't need plating,' Andy said.

'We'll give him a sedative and the cast will give enough support for it to heal. I'll write a referral for the orthopaedic surgeon for a check next week, and when he wakes up you can take him home and look after him.'

Chrissie sighed. 'Poor baby. He'll go berserk with boredom if he can't be a daredevil.' She looked at Montana. 'Sorry I have to leave you. So much for helping you settle in.'

'I'll be fine.' Montana shook her head. 'I've learnt the essentials this morning and if I need anything I can call Andy or talk to you on the phone. And Bill will be here after lunch when he starts his shift. I can save any questions I have for him.'

By eleven Montana was in charge of the hospital but there were no more moments of unusual interest for the rest of the day. Just two old dears in the medical end who wanted to know what had happened with the siren.

Andy brought Dawn over to her mother at lunch-time as Louisa was cooking up a storm for Ned's surprise party the following week, and they spent an agreeable half-hour discussing who would come to the party.

Montana was back home by four and was pleasantly satisfied with her first day.

When she walked in to the kitchen, Andy was there jiggling Dawn on his lap and Montana shook her head in disbelief.

'I can't believe how many times I've seen you today.'

Andy looked at Dawn. 'I know. Crazy, isn't it?'

Montana was confused at the undercurrents but couldn't pin down what disturbed her. 'One of us is.'

They smiled at each other and then Montana realised she was flirting. Where did she expect that to lead? Her baby was only four months old and her husband gone for just under a year.

Horrified with herself, she wanted to cry and scream and beat her chest that life was unfair and too confusing, but she battened down the urge. But she needed to get away from him.

'I'll take Dawn. Excuse me,' she said, and left the room rapidly with her daughter.

Andy watched her go.

Maybe it was wishful thinking but he had an idea what she was struggling with.

It was strange to be attracted to a person other than the one you'd promised to love for life.

He was finding it difficult himself and he'd

had longer than Montana to adjust to loss and change. Maybe it was all too new and too hard for both of them.

The night of Ned's seventieth birthday arrived and Montana decided she would enjoy the evening without regret.

Ned was a delight and she wished him a great party. She wouldn't bring any of her heartache to ruin his evening, though she'd probably be late because she still had a dilemma about what to wear.

She'd spent far too much time unconsciously fantasising about how Andy would look in his kilt and none about how to dress herself.

In the end she chose a black skirt and white lacy top with a frilled neckline. If it looked a little like it could go with a tartan cape, so what?

Ned was due back from his chess game at seven and the guests were arriving from six-thirty on to be in and hidden by seven.

Louisa had been cooking for weeks and Montana planned to slip into the kitchen to see if she could help with any last-minute chores.

She'd just settled Dawn down for a sleep when Andy knocked softly on her door.

'You there, Montana?' His voice was low but she had no problem distinguishing the words. Funny, that.

She felt her heart trip a little and she frowned at herself. She took a deep breath and opened her door.

She almost forgot to breathe out. He looked so incredible.

'Well? Say something.' She couldn't believe he was unsure. He didn't need to be nervous.

'Oh, my goodness,' was all she said, and even that came out muffled because her hand had flown up to cover her mouth.

Andy stared back anxiously. 'Do I look silly?'

Her heart swooped and dived in her chest like there was a big hand in there squeezing and chasing it around. 'Silly isn't a word that leaps to mind,' she said. She met his eyes and dragged her hand away and smiled. 'No. You look amazing. Fabulous. And very Scottish.'

'Och, aye, then.' He grinned and twirled his yellow and red kilt. 'I still can't decide whether to wear jocks or not.'

She blinked and her face flushed at the thought. 'You're kidding me.'

He grinned again. 'Yeah, but I had you worried.'

Kill that thought. But, of course, she couldn't. She felt like a kid waking up on her birthday. But that was silly. It was Ned's birthday.

'That's a relief. I was worried for the innocent children if you fall over later.'

'You are a hard woman, Montana Browne.' He may have said 'hard' but he'd said it softly and the meaning didn't correlate with the word.

Andy appeared to like what he saw of her outfit too. His gaze lingered and goose-bumps ran down her arms. She needed space and forced herself to move out of the danger zone.

'And you look cute in a skirt,' she said, 'but I have to go and see if I can do something for poor Louisa. She's worked herself up into a state.'

'A kilt, woman, not a skirt. Please.' He glanced at his watch. 'What about you and I take over the kitchen from Louisa and she can go and change and put on her make-up before Ned arrives? Chrissie has come over to meet people at the door and hide them in the library until seven.'

In the kitchen Louisa laughed so hard at the kilt that in the end Montana even felt sorry for Andy.

'Watch you don't lay an egg there, Louisa.' Andy pretended to be miffed. 'Off you go and pretty yourself up for seven. We'll look after your work here and meet you in the library at five to seven.'

Louisa scurried out, dragging off her apron as she went, but she still giggled.

Montana glanced at Andy's crestfallen face as she stirred the rice salad in a bowl. 'Poor Andy. She laughed at you.'

Andy scooped coleslaw into a large crystal dish. 'I prefer to think she laughed with me, if you don't mind.'

She placed a sprig of parsley in the middle of her bowl and then Andy's for decoration. 'I think you look wonderful.'

'That's all that matters, then.' He'd said it lightly but when Montana looked at him again he was watching her.

She turned away to the sink to hide her flushed

cheeks. There was more to that statement than she'd first realised.

'By the way…' He was right behind her when she turned back. He had a sprig of parsley in his hand and he held it over their heads. 'It's not mistletoe but it will do.'

'What—?' She didn't finish and he pulled her gently into his arms and kissed her. Only a gentle kiss but this time there was a hint of promise that he had further plans. She didn't know what she thought of that and there wasn't time to think about it now.

'I needed that for my bruised ego,' was all he said.

She frowned. He was getting a little too easy with his kisses. 'Glad I could be of service, but a little warning wouldn't go astray.'

Don't read too much into it, she told herself. 'We should move to the library because I think I just heard Joe's car arrive to drop off Ned.'

Andy looked horrified. 'You can hear outside noises while I kiss you?' He shook his head as he popped the salads into the fridge. 'That's not a good recommendation of my technique.'

'We will talk about your technique later.' Which is pretty darn good, she added silently. 'Let's go or we'll miss the surprise.'

They slipped into the dark library past Chrissie who raised her eyebrows at Andy's kilt, and then everyone was silent as they heard the front door open.

'Of course you can come in, Joe.' Ned sounded

jovial and Montana suspected he might even have had a whisky to help with his chess game.

He went on as another voice could be heard on the veranda. 'Louisa can always set another place at the table. Now, where is everybody?'

'In here, Ned,' Andy called out, and they waited in the darkness for the door to open.

It did so and a shaft of light preceded Ned's face as he peered into the room. 'Has the bulb blown?' he asked, and flicked the switch.

'Surprise!' Twenty smiling faces appeared with the light and Ned took a step back and clutched his chest.

'A dinna ken what you're doin' here.' He lapsed into broad Scots and Andy patted his back.

'It's all right, oldtimer. It's a surprise party for your seventieth. Don't have a heart attack on us.'

'Well, what do you expect? A bunch of noddies like you in the dark would scare anyone.'

He peered at the way Andy was dressed. 'Andy, me boy. You've found yourself a kilt. You look bonny.'

'In honour of you.' Andy rotated to show it off.

'I appreciate that. I really do. You should have had one sooner.' Ned looked around. 'Now, where's that lass of yours?'

'Would that be me?' Montana smiled and kissed Ned's cheek. 'Many happy returns, Ned.'

'Thank you, sweetheart.'

'Don't thank me. Louisa has been slaving in secret for weeks.'

He turned to Louisa with a soft smile. 'Now you are my true sweetheart.' Ned put his hand out to the older woman and pulled her forward.

'Dear Louisa. Thank you.' He planted a gentle kiss on his housekeeper's startled lips and winked at Andy.

The music started in the background, a Scottish reel that Ned loved, and he towed Louisa forward. 'I'm afraid I'm a bit slow in one hip but now that I'm a decent age I'll no let grass grow under my feet. Shall we dance, lass?'

Ned twirled a laughing Louisa into the middle of the floor and the party began.

Montana stepped back and watched with a smile on her face until Andy came up behind her and pulled her back against his body.

'We need to check the kitchen,' he said into her ear and Montana didn't know which sensation to register first. The feel of his hard body against her back or the fluttery jangle of nerves he'd sent to her stomach with his whispery breath. She shouldn't be registering either.

She pulled away and stood straight again. 'Lead the way. We can get the food out onto the table in the hall and open all the doors.'

Andy frowned and followed. 'Then we can talk about my technique.'

Chrissie came up behind them. 'What technique would that be, Andy?' There was a bubble of laughter in her voice and Montana stifled a giggle.

Andy was having a poor evening being the butt of everyone's jokes.

Andy had the answer. 'A new surgical tie, Chrissie. Where are you going?'

Chrissie looked surprised. 'I'm coming to help Montana in the kitchen, of course.'

Andy nodded as if he'd suspected she might be. 'Then I'm off to drink to Ned's health.'

But he slipped out to the veranda because suddenly he didn't feel like partying.

There'd been a few occasions when he'd thought that Montana felt the same way he did or at least had begun to be attracted to him. Then she would close up like a clam and he'd be back at square one.

He become way too attracted to the maddening woman to get himself out of the nowhere land he seemed stuck in.

In the three years since his wife had died he hadn't looked at another woman until Montana. She had broken through the shell around his heart with her courage and serenity and the last thing he wanted to do was damage that serenity by making a nuisance of himself.

He needed to proceed slowly for both of them but it was hard. Especially when he glimpsed the passionate woman he knew she'd be.

When he went back to the party half an hour later Montana was dancing with Chrissie's husband and he leant against the wall and watched.

What was it about this woman that affected him so?

Her dark hair was still confined in an ornate clasp and the slender column of her throat rose from her shoulders like the stem of flower. The hollow beneath her ear and her jaw made him want to draw her in and rest his fingers on that flushed delicate skin. Just to feel it. Inhale her scent there.

He pushed himself off the wall and was considering returning outside when she looked up, smiled and crooked her finger at him. 'Your wish is my command,' he murmured to himself, as he powerlessly moved towards her.

Chrissie's husband stepped back with a grin and suddenly Andy had what he wanted—Montana in his arms, and the chance to hold her close without needing an excuse.

She stepped into his embrace as if she'd been waiting for him, but that was wishful thinking on his part.

Either way, her body fitted perfectly with his, and he held her lightly, barely needing to guide her as their steps matched the dance movements.

'Where did you go?' she asked above the music. 'We looked for you after we finished in the kitchen.'

'Stargazing. But the view is just as magical in here. Did I mention you look beautiful?' You feel beautiful, he added silently, and as he leant down her subtle perfume was as intoxicating as he'd imagined it would be. Somehow he resisted the urge to brush that sensitive skin under her ear with his lips.

'I think you look magnificent in your kilt, Dr Buchanan.'

'Magnificent, eh? That sounds promising.'

'Let's just dance.' She leant her cheek against his chest and he gathered her closer and closed his eyes. She was right—they needed to just dance.

After the party, when all the revellers had departed and the mess had been cleaned up, Montana disappeared before he could say goodnight. But maybe that was better.

He went for a fast walk along the lake to clear—or was that cool?—his mind, but it didn't work.

Back in his room he dropped the kilt and shirt and, wrapping his towel around his waist, strode down the hallway to the bathroom.

Everyone else was in bed and probably sleeping the sleep of the innocent. He was anything but that.

Tonight he wanted Montana and he pulled back the screen and stepped into the shower, blasting his skin with an icy dousing from the shower. He shuddered as the onslaught beat against his chest and ran icily over his belly, but he knew it was the only way there was a chance he'd be able to sleep.

He twisted the tap to hot and then cold again and then hot and cold again until he stood at last with the cold water pelting him into submission.

He sighed, reached and turned the tap off, then slung the towel around his waist and took himself to bed.

CHAPTER EIGHT

A WEEK later Clare's results had come back positive for Huntington's disease, and the whole town reeled with shock.

Emma had gone into caring mode for her mother and was even reluctant to leave long enough to talk to Montana about her coming baby.

It was as if she didn't want to think about the future too much and by being busy she could ignore what was hanging over her mother's—and her own—head.

Montana could understand a tiny fraction of being busy to avoid things because she was ignoring a showdown with her own conscience.

She'd taken to spending long hours when Dawn was asleep in the evenings on her computer to assemble procedures and protocols for the running of the stand-alone caseload midwifery unit.

A lot of the paperwork she adapted from that she'd prepared before, which had been sent across by Misty from Westside. Apart from the state differences, the main area of organisation was in the transportation of women should medical need arise.

Andy was a general practitioner with his obstetric diploma so could give medical back-up prior to transfer, but they needed seamless access to an obstetric service for sick mums and babies.

The base would hopefully supply that but Montana needed to set up networking so everybody was happy.

It kept her out of Andy's way, plus exhaustion was good, and didn't leave enough time to think about how disloyal she'd been to Douglas, even if it was only in her mind as she approached a year since he had died.

It was indecently early for her to be even thinking of another man.

The first of May, a year since Douglas died, was a cold and rainy day at Lyrebird Lake. It fell on a Friday and she'd agreed to do a shift for Chrissie who wanted to go away for the weekend with her family.

She didn't mention the significance of the day to anyone at the Lake because she didn't know how she felt, though she had spoken to Misty and Mia that morning when they'd rung to see how she was.

At least she'd stayed busy with outpatients and when the shift was over she borrowed Louisa's car and drove herself and Dawn up the winding road to the lookout where she gazed out over the town.

A town that she realised she'd grown to love.

'Is it already a year since you left, Douglas?' she said to the sky, and shook her head in disbelief.

She cuddled Dawn against her and sighed. It didn't feel as though anyone was there.

She couldn't even imagine Douglas could hear her and she wanted to believe that was a good thing. He was at rest. He wasn't haunting her. He wanted her to get on with her life but she couldn't help the feeling of guilt.

The distant sound of another car as it climbed the hill penetrated her reverie and she turned to watch it park beside hers.

She'd known it was Andy even before she'd seen his vehicle.

He walked across to her and she wasn't sure if she was glad or sorry he had come.

'I've been worried about you all day and I'm sorry if I'm intruding.' His compassion made her want to weep all over him and she really didn't want to do that. She tried to talk but her throat was closed.

When she didn't answer he came to stand beside her and looked past her at the view. 'Just tell me to go and I will.'

Misty must have rung him. 'Stay. Maybe you can help. I'm just so confused that I feel this way when a year ago I thought I would never be happy again.'

He looked at her swiftly and then away, as if afraid of the answer. 'Are you happy?'

She sighed and accepted the truth. 'I love it here. Dawn is happy. Life shouldn't be this good only a year after Douglas's death.'

Andy rubbed his neck. 'What's the right time to start living after a loss like that?' He turned back to face her and she could see he felt strongly about this. 'Everyone is different. You knew to get away was the best thing for you and Dawn and I believe with all my being that you did the right thing.'

She looked into his face, and his eyes said that he did understand. Andy had always understood. 'I can't help feel it's too fickle of me to be almost healed. To want a new life for Dawn and I. To look at happy families and want that for us. He's only been gone a year.'

Andy nodded. 'For some people a new life might not come along for ten years but for others it arrives within months. There are no rules to say you haven't suffered enough. You just have to be strong enough to grab it when it comes.'

Late one afternoon Emma arrived at the doctors' house for another antenatal class.

'I'm glad you could come, Emma,' Montana said when Emma hugged her.

'I wanted to come.' She looked around the familiar room and then back at Montana. 'It is good to see you, too, and get out of the house.'

Montana followed her into the room. 'Sit. Unwind. How are your father and mother?'

They sat at the table where Montana had set up cold drinks and savoury biscuits, and Emma began to relax.

'Dad's pretty amazing, really. He's already made the house safer and easier to maintain for Mum, which has helped her cut back on accidents. He keeps telling her he loves her and he will love her for ever, no matter what.'

Emma's eyes filled up. 'If I have the gene then no one will have the chance to love me like that.' She paused and blinked away the tears. 'Because I won't let them.'

Montana could tell something had upset her badly. 'What has Tommy said?'

Emma threw her head up. 'He said his mother reckons we should terminate the pregnancy.' Her hands cupped protectively over her baby like they had the day Andy had diagnosed her mother. 'How can people say things like that about my baby?'

Montana sighed. Poor Emma. 'Some people say sad things when they're scared.' She squeezed Emma's hand. 'You'll have to pretend she didn't say it.'

Emma's lip quivered and Montana ached to be able to comfort her. 'There's a big chance you don't have the gene, Emma. Even if you do, your baby has just as big a chance not to have it.'

Emma brushed her hand across her eyes, scrubbing the wetness away. 'I'm not worried about me and it's too far away to think about when my child is thirty. It's when my baby is threatened now. But how could she even say that? Tommy's not even talking to her any more.'

'When your baby is born, Tommy's mother will want to be involved too, and should be. A grandchild is a wonderful joy in life. Tommy's mother is just not as strong as you at the moment and she will regret her comments when she loves your baby. But everything takes time.'

Emma nodded and Montana went on. 'In less than ten weeks your gorgeous baby will be here and you will be an awesome mother.'

Emma dropped her voice. 'I don't know anything about looking after a baby. How will I know what to do?'

Montana smiled. 'When you come in to have your baby we'll help you practise caring for it before you come home. Then we'll visit you at home and help with anything you need help with. But you'll learn fast because you'll love your baby.'

Montana lowered her voice. 'Don't underestimate that you still have your mother to help you learn to mother your baby as well.'

Emma nodded. 'I know. One of my friends' mothers was killed in the car three years ago. She said I'm lucky I still have my mum.'

She sniffed and visibly shook off her distress. 'And I really don't want to waste Mum's good times worrying about the not so good ones to come.'

She looked Montana in the eye. 'I am glad I

came because I can talk about things with you I can't say to other people and it helps me clear my brain.'

Montana hugged her. 'Your baby is one lucky little boy or girl.' She stepped back, brushed her eyes, and sniffed. 'I'd better blow my nose and get on with it, then. It's time we discussed labour.'

Andy had been sitting on the veranda and he couldn't help overhearing the conversation. Poor Emma. Poor Montana, because she was fond of Emma, too.

He felt like strangling Tommy's mother but instead he'd better go and see if he could talk some sense into her.

He had an hour and a half until Louisa served the evening meal. If he did half as well as Montana had with Emma, it would be worth it.

As he drove he shook his head at the amazing conversation he'd overheard. It made him see Montana again and what she'd brought to the Lake and to him.

If only he could use that same rationale with her in regard to getting on with life.

Her husband was dead and life was too precarious to waste opportunities like they had, but it was just too soon.

He could see how amazing those opportunities were for the two of them—now he needed her to see that.

He needed someone else to talk some sense into

her. It had been too long since he'd pursued a woman with a view to commitment and obviously he was going about it all wrong.

Maybe he should ring his sister tonight, get some advice or see when she was coming out, even if he had to fly down and get her himself.

CHAPTER NINE

THAT Friday, when Montana had finished the first well-women's clinic held at the hospital, Andy appeared.

He allowed himself the luxury of admiring her as she organised her desk.

Her hair was tied back in a shiny clasp and several dark wisps tickled her cheek. He wanted to brush them back with his fingers and make her see how good the two of them would be together.

Now that he'd come to realise how much Montana meant to him, he needed her to see it too.

'Montana, a question?' he said softly, not wanting to startle her, and Montana looked up at his voice. The unguarded, welcoming smile on her face gave him some hope at least.

She straightened and brushed the hair away from her cheek. 'Hello, there, Dr Buchanan. Yes?'

He walked over and looked at the list of patients she'd seen that day. It was a long one. Obviously there were a fair proportion of the townswomen who had avoided their yearly checks until Montana had arrived.

As he stood beside her he could just catch the faintest hint of the lavender soap she used. Going into the bathroom at the house was always a struggle after Montana had been in there because that scent left too vivid a picture in his mind to relax with.

She stretched her neck to look up at him and he was tempted to kiss those pouting lips she teased him with.

'We're to be formal, then, Sister Browne? And I was going to ask you something very informal.'

Her beautiful brows went up and he smiled and went on. 'It's your first clinic. Let's celebrate at the only restaurant in town tonight for dinner. Just the two of us.'

'Like a date?' She was teasing him again. What the hell? It was better than nothing.

'Not *like* a date.' He paused and she tilted her head and he could see she'd missed the point. 'As a real date. Dinner, dancing, table service. A date. Say yes.'

Montana blinked. 'They have dancing?'

He smiled. 'They have a romantic opera collection on CD and a handkerchief-sized dance floor.'

She looked away and he couldn't catch the expression he'd wanted to see.

'Have Louisa mind Dawn, do you mean?' She turned back to him and he watched different emotions cross her face as she considered the logistics.

Why couldn't she just say yes and work it out later?

Then she did. 'I'd like that, Andy. If Louisa isn't busy, it would be nice to get dressed up a little and have a meal out.'

'With me.' He clarified the situation because he needed her to get it.

'With you.' She smiled at him as the idea grew. Just like the pleasure that expanded in his own chest. It felt good to hear her say yes.

'Yes, please.' She said again. 'What time?'

'Say six-thirty for seven.' Already he was planning. 'We can have a leisurely meal, a few turns around the floor.' He wanted to relive that feeling of Montana in his arms. 'We'd still not be home too late for Dawn.'

Maybe walk along the lake afterwards and watch the submarine races, he thought, but didn't add that.

This was such a good idea. Misty had suggested it and it sent the message he wanted to make. A date shifted the platonic colleague thing into a whole new area.

He hoped so because the last few weeks he'd been going quietly insane.

Montana was ready early because she'd learnt that babies tended to have last-minute moments of unusual interest and she didn't want to keep Andy waiting.

Andy found her in the kitchen with Dawn at six-fifteen, dressed and ready, and she blushed at the way his eyes lit up when he saw her.

She'd pampered herself in the bathroom and then spent extra time drying her hair so that it shone and bounced freely around her neck—a big change, as she rarely left her hair down.

Tonight it had seemed like the thing to do. Her apricot blouse left her shoulders bare and the floral skirt swirled when she twirled in her strappy sandals. All those things—and the way Andy looked at her—made her feel especially feminine tonight and it was a giddy feeling she wasn't used to.

Dawn waved them goodbye, with a little help from Louisa, and they walked under the streetlights to the restaurant. The breeze from the lake seemed especially soft tonight.

Andy caught her hand and held it and she left her fingers there, warm and secure in his, and tried to ignore the flutter of tension that level of commitment left her with.

The Paragon, the only restaurant in Lyrebird Lake, was run by Angelo and Angelina, an eccentric Italian couple who supplemented the menu they loved to serve with a sideline pizza take-away.

In the main restaurant, to Montana's surprise, the room was dim with dripping candles in basketed Chianti bottles and red-checked tablecloths.

Romantic Italian opera played softly in the background and she smiled at the memory of Andy's forewarning.

The only other couple in the room were being served their meal with a voluble flourish as Montana and Andy arrived, and the little Italian looked torn between the two tasks.

'We'll seat ourselves, Angelo. No hurry, please,' Andy said and ushered Montana to a secluded corner where a sheaf of long purple roses lay across the table.

He smiled and pulled her chair out then tilted his head towards the Italian.

'Angelo likes to explain the meal when he serves it, and I didn't want to spoil his fun.'

Montana lifted the roses before she sat down. Andy being thoughtful again? She inhaled the exquisite scent. 'Did you send these in for me?'

'From Clare's garden. I picked them up earlier. I swear she has every colour you could imagine.'

Her brows drew together as a memory teased her. 'I'm sure you mentioned a special meaning for purple roses before.'

'Later,' he said, and seated her with such care she felt pampered and revered, as if she were a movie star. Secretly she thought Andy could hold his own with anyone on the big screen so she had the right dinner partner.

She brushed her hand over the cutlery, as if the coldness of the silver would rid her head of silly thoughts. Or at least bring her back to earth.

The tantalising aroma of herbs and garlic and

mozzarella made Montana mouth water and she forgot about Andy's reason for purple roses.

For the first time in months she realised how hungry she was. It was a classical Italian restaurant but there was nothing clichéd about the aroma of the food and she couldn't wait to see the menu.

In fact, she hadn't really been interested in what she'd eaten since Douglas had died. Maybe that was all a part of feeling so alive and vital tonight.

She smiled at Andy as he settled on the opposite side of the table. 'Thank you for bringing me here.'

'My pleasure, madam.' He bowed and gave her one of those gorgeous hundred-watt smiles that made her whole body glow before he flicked his napkin onto his lap.

Montana settled back in her chair and sighed as she looked around. 'This is wonderful, Andy. The food looks and smells authentic, and Angelo could be in any restaurant in Rome.'

They both looked across at the dapper Italian in his black shiny trousers, bow-tie and white apron. His hands gesticulated floridly as he explained intricate details to the other couple.

'He's a gem. Believe it or not, Angelo grew up around here. His parents immigrated many years ago and ran a huge property about fifty kilometres out of town.

'Angelo travelled to Italy to study under a master chef in Rome. There he met Angelina, who is also a chef. They had four sons in five years but came back when his parents needed help on the station.'

He looked fondly at the little Italian. 'Now the boys run the station and Angelo and his wife can do what they love. Cook. Here he comes.'

Andy stood up and Angelo pumped Andy's hand as if he'd never let it go.

'Dr Andy, and your beautiful lady. Welcome to my Paragon.'

He put two menus down on the table and leaned towards Montana as if he had a secret to share. 'He saved my life, this doctor. I would be dead but for him. But here I am and my beautiful wife and I will prepare you food from the gods.'

He paused and spread his arms. 'What's mine is yours.' He beamed at them both. 'Now, tell me, Andy, who is this beautiful lady?'

'This is Montana. A midwife. Perhaps your son's sons can be born at the Lake now that she is here.'

'Sì. This would be excellent.' He nodded and smiled again. 'Maybe a granddaughter for my wife one day.'

Andy looked him up and down. 'You're looking well. How are Angelina and the boys?'

Angelo patted his round stomach. 'I am too well. My Angelina you will see later, she is beautiful, and my boys are multiplying. Already I have six grandsons. How can a man be so fortunate? Eh?'

He pointed at Andy and said to Montana, 'Relax. Enjoy. He is a good man.'

Montana smiled. 'I know.'

'I will be back.' Angelo nodded, smiled and left them.

'He's great, Andy. So is this place. I had no idea, judging from the outside, it looks like an ordinary pizza parlour.'

'Wait till you taste the food.' He kissed his fingers and grinned. They ordered after much consultation with Angelo, who wouldn't allow their first choice.

'You must be brave!' he said sternly.

Angelo brought them a chilled bottle of sparkling Shiraz from a boutique vineyard. 'On the house. This is from my cousin in the Hunter Valley and I save it for special occasions. For you. The best wine in Australia. Taste.'

Angelo poured the deep plum-coloured wine and it winkled in their glasses like the fizzing atmosphere that had been building up between Montana and Andy since they'd sat down.

Montana's first sip made her eyes open wide and Angelo clapped his hands in delight.

'See!'

'My goodness.' She sipped again. The berry-flavoured Shiraz bubbled and rolled on her tongue and this time she closed her eyes to concentrate. 'Amazing. My first sparkling red and I'm already addicted.'

Angelo left them and Montana looked up to see Andy watching her. A tiny smile tilted the corner of his lips.

It made the warmth steal into her face again and she wished she had a fan to wave and cool her cheeks. 'What?'

'You!' He tilted his head. 'Watching you makes me smile. You make me feel good.'

The words were simple but there was no doubting his sincerity and he followed them with his hand across the table to capture her fingers.

'I'm falling for you, Montana, and it's time I told you that. So I give you purple roses.'

He brushed the blooms at the side of her plate gently. 'Love at first sight. And I thought that was a myth.'

She could feel the shock reflected in her face and he sat back. Her fingers slid from his and he smiled ruefully.

'It's OK. Don't look so shaken. That's all. It's my problem, not yours. I just wanted you to know in case you could begin to think about us building a life together some time in the future.'

He leaned forward and topped up their glasses to help fill the silence that had fallen. She glanced around the room to see if it all still looked the same because suddenly everything was different for her.

Nothing had drastically changed in the environment but things had certainly tilted with her and Andy.

She picked up her glass and swirled the liquid, not sure what to say.

It wasn't just moving on from the past, and

Douglas, and how she saw her future. It was Andy, fearlessly facing the same and moving on, unlike her. He was incredibly brave. And she didn't know if she could match that bravery.

The big part of her was terrified that now it had been said and there was no going back, while the other was releasing bursts of tiny bubbles of excitement like the Shiraz in the glass she stared into.

'Don't stress. Enjoy the meal.' Andy's voice drifted softly over her, just like it had when she'd been on the mountain, and she remembered who he was. This was Andy. She was safe.

'Just think about it for a while,' he said. 'We're still friends.'

She raised her eyes and nodded her head. He was right. He didn't expect her to respond in kind in this instant. She couldn't.

With relief she watched Angelo approach with crusty bruschetta and the Italian's smile lightened her preoccupation.

The conversation between them turned to the hospital and the new maternity wing. The hunt for staff looked to be easier than expected when word had spread about the caseload midwifery programme.

They discussed a spate of sick children in the last week and gradually she relaxed and began to enjoy herself again.

But now, deep inside, a tiny flicker of joy had ignited to quietly gain in strength as she relaxed, as if to shine too quickly it might be extinguished. Or maybe that was the wine.

The meal was accompanied by a visit from Angelo's wife, a tall, black-eyed seductress who Montana thought could never have borne four strapping sons.

'And she ruled them with a rod of iron. A very strong lady is our Angelina,' Andy said later when she'd gone.

'This town becomes more interesting and exciting the more I see of it.'

'Good,' said Andy, and she could see he was pleased, although he said no more.

They skipped dessert to savour a liqueur that Angelo insisted they try. Inky black Sambucca brought in tiny shot glasses with coffee beans that Angelo insisted on lighting, whirling, extinguishing and ordering them to sip.

The heated liqueur slid like black gold down her throat and Montana hoped Dawn wouldn't mind that she'd had two drinks tonight.

When Andy suggested they dance she knew it would feel different now. He stood beside her chair and held out his hand to help her up and she felt like a princess again. How did he do that? Create such magic?

When he circled her waist she closed her eyes and leant against him. His shirt was a thin barrier to the firm muscles under her cheek and his lips near her neck made her sensitive to every breath that he took.

Amazingly their steps matched as they swayed to the music—amazing because no part of her brain could be spared for such a mundane thing as rules of a dance while Andy held her.

And he offered so much more.

On their walk home, when Andy suggested a stroll around the lake, she demurred because she was already heavy with desire and needed time to consider the implications of Andy's stated intention. So they went home to Dawn and their separate rooms.

At least she knew how he felt, Andy consoled himself later as he stepped into the flagellation of the cold shower, though he wouldn't mind a warm end to the night instead of a freezing finish before bed.

For Montana there was a lot to think about.

It was time to consider life after Douglas without guilt. Without apologising for being alive when he wasn't. She acknowledged to herself she had loved her husband until the end.

But she and Dawn weren't meant to be lonely and alone.

She needed a man to talk to and she so loved talking to Andy. Dawn needed a good father and Andy would slip into that role with barely a ripple—had already slipped into that role beautifully.

Andy would be a man to learn and live with and grow older with. He could so easily be that one person in the world to spend her life with, as she would be his.

She missed that. She missed a lot of things.

She loved the way Andy had shown her tonight how special he found her. The roses, the romance, his obvious pleasure in her pleasure. The smoulder in his eyes when he looked at her. And the hardest part was that she knew he would be a wonderful lover. As generous in bed as out, and that thought brought a flush to her skin that heated her right down to her toes.

If she started to think of Andy's strong neck and broad chest and those glorious shoulders and arms, she'd be a basket case.

If she was honest with herself, she'd admit she wanted to be seduced by Andy. Feel his hands on her skin. That had been the main factor in refusing to walk by the lake tonight. She'd wanted distance before she irrevocably committed herself, and if he'd leant on her tonight she'd have been unable to say no.

And the final reason she held back was the realisation she'd fallen in love with Andy and she was terrified it was a different, more complete love than that she had shared with Douglas.

But suddenly time to spend together deserted them.

By May the birthing centre application had been assessed and passed for their first birth.

The wing had been furnished like a home, not a hospital. Montana had begun the antenatal clinic and staff had been finalised. All they needed was a woman in labour.

Along with her administration days there seemed little time to spend with Andy. At least new staff had been found in two young midwives whose husbands worked at the mine.

Sara and Sue couldn't believe their luck at finding their dream jobs. Though not long graduated, both had loads of experience in a tertiary-affiliated birth centre in Brisbane, and were very happy to work with the base hospital whenever they needed to transfer a patient.

Each would work two shifts on call and two off and Montana would be the second person when birth was imminent.

More midwives were needed but there was no hurry. Montana doubted they would be run off their feet in the beginning.

By June Sara and Sue had accepted four women each on their case loads, which meant the women visited the unit for antenatal care with more visits as they drew closer to their due dates. As yet they hadn't had to pass any women with complications to Andy to refer on to the base obstetricians.

The first baby was due at the end of June and the three midwives carried their mobile phones everywhere, even where reception proved tricky.

Montana planned to caseload only with Emma until Dawn was older, and that left her free to be second on call when needed.

Today was Montana's day for Emma to be checked.

'So how are you keeping, Emma?' Montana let down the blood-pressure cuff on her arm as she studied Emma's face.

Emma shrugged miserably. 'I'm OK. Baby kicks a lot and now I'm getting heartburn after I eat all the time.'

'When you have baby, that will go away. Try smaller meals. Give your tummy time to empty before you drink anything. That will stop the acid contents splashing up through the floppy door leading from your tummy into your throat.'

'Why have I got a floppy door now?' Emma sounded just a little fed up and Montana sympathised with the tiredness of late pregnancy.

'It's all the fault of those muscle-loosening hormones. Your body can't pick and choose between muscles in your pelvis and muscles in your stomach, but your body is preparing itself for birth. Remember you can hurt your back easily now, too, as muscles can over-stretch.'

'I'm sick of me. How's Dawn?' Emma wanted to know. Emma had become fond of Montana's baby.

Montana smiled. 'She's rolling over onto her tummy and back again and puts everything into her mouth. And she loves having conversations with Andy. He talks, she gurgles and then he talks and she shrieks. It's so funny. You'll have to come and visit again.'

'I'd like that.'

'You and Tommy are coming to the class tonight, aren't you?'

'You bet. I want to see Andy in front of a class.'

That night Montana ran the first antenatal night class ever in Lyrebird Lake, with four women and their men as well as Emma and Tommy on a revision course.

The sessions proved popular, especially as the husbands and partners had never had the chance to attend before.

Andy gave descriptions of labour complications from the medical aspect and even enjoyed himself. They discussed reasons for transfer out of the centre to the base hospital and talked about premature labour and antenatal medical complications as well.

By the end even Tommy said he was glad he'd come.

The first of July heralded the cooler weather and when Montana carried Dawn in to a late breakfast Andy had a surprise for them both.

He'd tied pink balloons around Dawn's high chair and a handmade card sat on her little tray table.

'Happy birthday, Dawn.' The others clapped as Montana carried her daughter in and she stopped in the doorway.

'You're all mad. It's not her birthday for another six months.'

Andy sniffed. 'It's her half-birthday and it's the first of July. I declare a Lyrebird Lake holiday because it's Sunday.' Andy swooped on Dawn and flew her over to her chair to see the balloons.

Dawn cackled in delight and waved her hands as she tried to capture Andy's face. Louisa stood with her hands in her apron pockets, clapping her hands, and even Ned had appeared early to be part of the festivities.

Montana looked around at the caring and warmth of these people who had taken her into their home. At a time when she'd needed unobtrusive support they'd given unstintingly, and she could feel the sting of tears. Andy would have arranged this. She forced her tears back because the last thing they needed was to think they had upset her.

She sniffed. 'Who would have thought today was such a momentous day? How could I have forgotten my own daughter's half-birthday?'

Ned tut-tutted.

Andy nodded sagely. 'You may have had other things on your mind but it's OK.'

Louisa bustled up to lift up a pink-iced cake complete with a picture of a sunrise on it and 'Half' written in icing.

'Oh, my.' Montana peered at the cake. 'It's incredible. But won't we all be sick if we have that for breakfast?'

'You could squeeze in a wee piece if you eat it after eggs,' Ned declared sagely.

Even Dawn enjoyed her cake by mushing it gloriously between her fingers, finger-painting her tray and then smearing icing and crumbs onto her mouth. Her little pink tongue darted busily as she crowed and played.

Louisa hovered with a dishcloth, not sure how far and wide Dawn was capable of spreading the mess, while the others backed off.

After the party, Andy tucked Dawn against his side and drew Montana out onto the veranda and into the swing seat.

The three of them swung gently and gazed across the lake. 'So where would you like to go for Dawn's birthday?' Andy said.

'So this day will get even better?' she teased.

Andy's eyes twinkled wickedly and she blushed and looked away. They really hadn't had time for themselves and she knew Andy wanted to talk again about their future. It was time she met him halfway. 'We'd love a picnic.'

Montana looked across at the lake and then up to the hills. 'I hear there's a waterfall halfway down the creek.'

Andy considered the idea. 'I did say that but it's more of a rapid than a waterfall. It's pretty and the track at the top isn't too far from the road. I could easily carry Dawn and an esky if you bring the hamper and a rug.'

He thought about it some more. 'There's a great clearing not far from the old antimony mine.'

Dawn would love her first picnic. 'Sounds perfect. Are you on call?'

Andy nodded. 'But higher up there's mobile service. And we could take more cake.'

Montana patted her stomach. 'Not if I want to fit into my jeans.'

Andy raised his eyebrows in mock censure. 'There's always room for the good things in life. Trust me.'

CHAPTER TEN

THREE hours later, because like any mother it seemed to take Montana so long to organise any expedition with Dawn, they finally found the waterfall. A waist-deep pool beckoned beyond and Andy answered the call even though it was quite cool.

Montana dangled Dawn's feet at the edge and tried not to stare at Andy as he encouraged her to come in.

Droplets sparkled in his hair and off his strong throat as he played in the water and pretended to splash her. His green eyes wickedly seduced her while he spoke silly talk to Dawn.

When she refused for the third time he dived under the water once more and then lifted himself effortlessly onto the smooth boulder beside Montana.

'I haven't been here for ages. I have no idea why not. I'd forgotten how much I love it.'

He was close and wet and half-naked and she wanted to chase rivulets of water down his chest just to feel the firmness beneath her fingers. Instead she said, 'It's good to see you relaxed. You work so hard week in, week out. How do you keep your good humour? That's what I want to know.'

'Great friends. Great people.' He shrugged. 'It's not hard.'

She realised his kindness never seemed stretched. Like today and the party he'd organised for Dawn.

'You should have more time off, Andy,' she said. 'Look after yourself, instead of arranging parties for stray mothers and babies.'

He smiled crookedly. 'I will when I have a reason to take time off.'

He said the words lightly but Montana felt they were directed at her and suddenly the little oasis seemed warmer and more private.

She shifted topic to allow herself time to adjust. 'How did you remember it was Dawn's birthday?'

Andy shook his head, denying it had been hard. 'Forget the day you and Dawn came into my life?' Andy looked across at her baby dozing now on her mother's lap. 'Forget the magic on the mountain on New Year's Day?' he said softly, and his words brought back the serenity of that morning.

Then he leant across and kissed her cheek and she could see he really did remember that day with emotion. 'You were amazing.'

She found herself leaning towards him and his long fingers stroked her jaw and drew her nearer.

Just the feel of his warm strength splayed across her cheek and the caress of his thumb sent sensations tumbling into her stomach and chest, and she couldn't help but close her eyes. She didn't see his mouth coming but she'd known it would happen. Wanted it to happen.

His lips brushed at hers with gently swooping sips of first one lip and then the other and then he captured her in a timeless seduction that drew the breath from her in tiny gasps of air and she held onto the back of his head in a quest to stay connected with his mouth.

The sensations caused the world to recede and Dawn didn't like the lack of attention. She squirmed in Montana's lap and the moment drifted away, as did Andy's mouth, and Montana sat back.

'Perhaps you should go to your room,' he said softly to Dawn, and smiled ruefully. 'Your mother and I are talking.'

He stood up. 'I guess it is her birthday, not mine.' Andy gathered up his clothes. 'I'll dress then unpack the hamper.'

Montana watched him go and wondered if there was an end to his patience. Maybe he was too patient!

They spent the rest of the afternoon discussing their childhoods and important people in their lives while Dawn played happily with shiny stones she couldn't pick up and watched the activity of nature around the pool.

At two they packed and drove home and not long after Andy went out on a call.

Montana dozed with Dawn on the big bed in her room, but pictures and memories of Andy crowded her mind. Was she wasting her life? Could she be happy with Andy? Would Andy love Dawn as a father?

Yes, of course. To all of them. So why, why couldn't she just say yes to Andy? Why this ridiculous hesitation and crushing load of guilt about Douglas?

Again she examined the concept that perhaps she hadn't loved Douglas as she realised she loved Andy, and that made her feel a hundred times more unfaithful to her dead husband.

If it had almost killed her to lose Douglas, what if she married Andy and fell more deeply in love every minute?

What of her soul should anything happen to Andy? How would she ever survive?'

The clarity of that fear had her sitting up on the edge of the bed and her heart pounded in her chest. Maybe that fear was larger than the fear of loneliness and of forgetting Douglas. It was scary to think it might be.

She buried her head under her pillow.

The phone call came through at four-thirty in the afternoon from Tommy.

'Montana?' His voice faded in and out with poor reception and Montana walked to the window.

'Tommy, is that you?' She couldn't rationalise

the reason but a cold chill ran down her neck at the sound of his voice.

'Emma's missing and I've looked and looked.'

Montana frowned. 'What do you mean, missing?'

'She went for a walk and didn't come back.' There was a thread of panic in Tommy's voice.

Montana glanced at the clock. 'Have you told her father?'

'He's at the mill with the brothers in the bush and I can't get through to him.' Tommy paused and then the words came in a rush. 'She's been acting strange and I'm worried.'

Montana squeezed the phone in her hand until her fingers whitened. 'I'm sure she's fine, Tommy. Probably just forgot the time.'

'She left after breakfast and she'd not back yet. She didn't take anything to eat.'

The dread inside Montana increased. 'Give me your number and I'll ring you back.'

Montana tried Andy's mobile but he was out of range and when she tried the hospital Chrissie said he was in a distant gully visiting an old man in a shack.

Ned had a distressed patient so she couldn't ask his advice and even Bob, the policeman, had been seconded to give evidence in court. Montana didn't know who else to contact.

She rang Tommy back. 'Did she say where she was going? Or give any hints?'

'Just that she needed to go for a walk. She can't

have gone far 'cause she's pretty big and waddles. She likes to sit in the gully near the mine because there's a creek but I looked there already.'

Montana tried to think. 'Have you rung all her friends?'

'Yep. Even the unfriendly ones. Nobody has seen her today.' Tommy had actually done well with his sleuthing.

Montana's brain raced. 'Was she upset when you talked to her this morning?'

'Yep,' he said. 'She's been getting queerer every day.' Montana felt like shaking him and asking why he hadn't mentioned something before this.

That wouldn't help and she needed Tommy thinking clearly, not upset by her censure. 'Fine. I'll have a drive around in the car, Tommy, and see if I can see her. Do you know if she has her mobile phone?'

'No.' Brief and non-explanatory, and she waited for him to elaborate. He didn't.

Frustration had her grit her teeth. 'No, she doesn't have her phone or, no, you don't know?'

'Don't know.' Tommy began to sound frightened at the unmistakable thread of concern in Montana's voice.

'Fine.' Montana drew a deep breath and calmed her urge to scream. 'I'll send a message to Andy with your number and he'll ring you as soon as he's back in mobile range.'

She ran through the options in her mind. 'Tell him what you've told me and that I'll drive to the mine and park my car and walk back to town from there. You come from the bottom up with Andy. It will be dark soon so I'd better go.'

The relief in Tommy's voice was palpable. 'Thanks, Montana.'

Montana rubbed her neck, a trait she'd obviously picked up from Andy. 'You did the right thing, ringing me, Tommy. Now, stay in range so Andy can ring you.'

Montana found Emma, tear-stained and terrified, just as the sun went down, midway between the mine and town. She'd twisted her ankle and her waters had broken.

Montana gathered her in her arms and hugged her, so pleased to see her alive because she'd been having some dark and dismal thoughts as she'd called out in the bush.

Emma clutched Montana's hand and pushed it low down on her stomach. 'I haven't any real pains yet but the five-minute tightenings are getting worse. It's awfully sore in here.'

Montana spread her fingers around Emma's belly button and felt the tautness rock hard against her hand. It felt like a contraction to her.

She glanced at her watch in the gathering gloom. Five-thirty. It would be pitch black by six. Shame it wasn't summer.

'We need to contact Andy.' Montana drew her phone from her jeans.

Emma nodded her head vigorously. 'Yes, please.'

Montana tried and then stood up and tried again. No signal on the phone. She resisted the impulse to throw the offending article into the creek.

'Look, Emma, I'll have to climb back up the hill and try for coverage, OK?'

'No. Don't leave me.' Emma turned her tear-stained face towards her and clutched Montana's hand. The fear in her eyes twisted Montana's heart.

'It's OK, Em. I'm not leaving you.' She eased her hand out of Emma's. 'I'll be five minutes, maximum ten. I'll talk to Andy and scoot down to you again. Can you cope with that?'

Emma swallowed. 'OK. But don't be longer, 'cause I'm scared and I need you here.'

Montana kissed the top of her head. 'I'll be as quick as I can. Sit on the rug I brought. At least it will keep the dampness from the ground getting to you.'

'Don't turn your own ankle,' Emma said with a weak attempt at humour.

Montana smiled. 'You're terrific. Back soonest.' Montana jogged up the path and tried not to think about all the spiders that would be preparing their webs for the night. After only a few minutes she had one bar of reception on her phone and she sent a little prayer of thanks skywards.

When she pressed in Andy's number the engaged signal had her mumbling under her breath in frustration. She disconnected and climbed a few feet higher.

Unexpectedly the phone rang in her hand and, startled, she allowed it to slide from her fingers and fall to the ground, where it bounced down between two rocks in a crevice just out of reach. Then it rang again.

'Damn,' she muttered. She'd have to lie down on the ground and slide her arm between two rocks and feel around for the phone. Her skin crawled at the thought of what else could be in the dark under the rock.

'I don't believe this,' she said out loud as the phone rang again, but the glow from the screen helped and the vibration made it easy to pick the right object.

She shuddered as she stood up and brushed herself down with one hand as she flicked open the phone with her other.

'Montana?' Andy's voice echoed reassuringly in her ear and she'd never been so pleased to hear anybody's voice. She drew a deep breath and calmed her racing heart.

'Andy.' She had to take another breath before she could talk again. 'I've found her. She's fine but five minutes away from me with no reception so I have to get back to her.'

'Are you all right?'

'I'm fine. Just dropped the phone in the dark down a hole and had to fish it out. Yuk.'

She could hear the smile in his voice. 'OK. Well done. Where are you?'

She shut her eyes for a moment and pictured Emma's position. 'It took me thirty minutes to walk from the mine down the hill along the creek. We're beside the creek and she's hurt her ankle and can't walk.'

Montana paused.

He'd love this. Not. 'By the way, she's ruptured her membranes and having five minutely contractions.'

There was a moment's silence while he digested that. Then he said, 'Of course she has. You do have moments of unusual interest.' Understatement.

Then he went on. 'Nothing we can do about that. I had an idea that's where you would be and I'm halfway there.'

Just like his sister, she thought. 'Family premonitions?' It was so reassuring to know he was close.

'Misty would be proud of me. We'll come up from the bottom. See you soon.'

'Soonest.' She looked at the phone as she shut it and thanked the mobile-phone god for being there.

When Montana skidded to a halt in a shower of pebbles beside Emma she could see the labour would wait for no man, not even Andy.

Emma turned anguished eyes towards Montana

and moaned. She moistened her lips with her tongue, and sighed at the end of the pain, just like Montana had said to do in the classes. 'I'm going to have my baby here, aren't I?'

Montana peered into her face in the gloom. 'You told me you weren't going to have your baby on a mountain.'

Emma sniffed. 'It's only a hill.'

Montana wanted to hug her. 'Well, that doesn't count, then. Besides, I think we'd be better to wait to christen our new birthing unit, don't you think?'

Emma grimaced. 'Would love to but I don't think I can wait.'

Montana re-evaluated their position. 'If that happens, it's not a tragedy. Women are designed to have babies and at least we have a rug and Andy is on his way with Tommy. Obviously you like the great outdoors and your baby will probably be a bushie too.'

She met Emma's eyes and hoped her gaze was rock solid with belief. 'We can manage. I did and you will.'

'How many people,' Emma said crossly and drew a panting breath, 'do you know...' she breathed again '...who had babies in the wild when they meant to have them in hospital?'

Emma glared and Montana smiled to herself. That crossness sounded like transition at the end of first-stage of labour.

'Um. Just me and maybe you.' She rubbed

Emma's arm. 'Hang in there. I'm here. Andy and Tommy are coming. Try to relax and enjoy the fact you'll meet your baby very soon.'

'I'm having a ball.' Emma grimaced and tried to smile then her tears began to well again. 'That's why I went for the walk. Mum told me today that she'd known her nana had had Huntington's and she'd blocked it out. We had a fight when I asked why she didn't tell me earlier.'

'Poor Emma.' Montana squeezed her hand.

'It was really dumb of me because Mum's got enough on her plate without me being hard to get along with. I just got so scared for my baby I wanted to get away and think.'

Her eyes implored Montana to understand. 'I didn't think the baby would come today. I wish I hadn't come out.'

'Hey. No more self-blame. If your baby comes today then so be it. It was your baby's decision. Let it come with you happy to see him or her. OK?'

Emma nodded and then she flinched at a rustle in the bushes. 'What was that?'

Montana frowned and tried to see in the gloom. There was still some light but it was too early for the moon and they were under trees. 'It's not a big noise so it isn't Andy. Probably a little creature frightened by us invading its home.'

The rustle came again and then suddenly, from the bush, a mobile phone rang briefly and then stopped.

They both froze and Montana pulled her phone from her pocket and stared at it. No call had been missed and she hadn't felt any vibration. 'Have you got your phone, Emma?'

Emma's voice shook. 'Not with me.'

The phone rang again from the bush next to them and they both stared. Then a sweet, melodious warble drifted from beneath the leaves and a small brown feathered bird strutted out to stare at them with its long lacy plumed tail dragging behind in the twilight.

It stared, strutted, and lifted its plume until feathers stood up behind him like a miniature silver harp, just like a small brown peacock on show.

'It's a lyrebird,' Emma whispered.

'He's gorgeous.' Montana couldn't believe they'd been so lucky.

As if satisfied that homage had been paid, the bird turned and with a shimmy of feathers it strolled back into the bush and disappeared.

'It was the phone. That's awesome.' Emma's hand slid down to her belly and she sighed again. 'Here comes another one.'

Montana rested her hand on Emma's shoulder. Not rubbing, just resting there to give her strength. 'Don't be afraid.'

Emma's voice sounded distant. 'Strangely, I'm not.' She smiled at Montana. 'Any more.' Then the pain came again.

CHAPTER ELEVEN

ANDY found them ten minutes later, his arrival preceded by the sudden silence of the evening creatures. Tommy followed and as they entered the clearing Emma turned her eyes to Montana.

'It's too late,' she said. 'I'm scared.' And pushed.

Montana wasn't as philosophical about the impending birth as she'd like either, and she wasn't sure why, but was fervently glad Andy had arrived in time.

'Don't be scared. You're safe.' Andy's calm voice settled over all of them and even Tommy lost his end-of-the-world face and stopped muttering.

Andy patted Tommy's back as he moved closer to Emma. 'Nice and easy, Emma. What more could you want? Tommy, Montana and I will cheer you on and your baby will be fine.'

Montana listened with relief. It was funny how she could handle the thought of her own birth in the bush, but for Emma she was suddenly very frightened.

Andy had brought the emergency delivery kit and at least they had the bare essentials and Montana's rug. But she was very glad Andy was with them.

The next pain built and as the evening deepened the first signs of the baby could be seen.

Montana loved this moment and she glanced across at Andy, who had his hand resting on Emma's shoulder as he gently encouraged her.

Tommy held Emma's hand and as night descended, Grace Isobel Victoria was born as crickets chirped and night birds called and to the sound of a distant mobile phone.

Baby Grace entered the world into Montana's caring hands and shortly after her first cry, another baby echoed from the bush.

'What was that?' Tommy's head twisted from side to side and Emma and Montana laughed softly.

'Later,' Montana said softly, and dried Grace quickly with the small towel Andy had brought with the kit. She laid the newborn gently skin to skin on her mother's breast so that she could stay warm with Emma's heat and hear her heartbeat.

'A girl. We've got a daughter,' Tommy whispered for all of them, and he squeezed Emma's hand and kissed her forehead and Montana felt relieved tears prick her eyes as she ensured that Emma's third stage of labour was complete.

Andy listened briefly to Grace's lungs and pronounced all well as Montana tucked the blanket over mother and baby and sat back on her heels.

She stripped off the gloves Andy had given her and glanced across to catch Andy's eyes. She found him watching her.

His eyes seemed darker in the evening light and his smile seemed a little strained, but he spoke warmly to Emma. 'You were fabulous, Emma. Well done.'

He looked at Montana. 'Let's give them some space. Emma and Tommy should be fine for a minute while we give them a moment alone with their daughter.'

'Of course,' Montana agreed.

Andy paused before stepping away. 'We could go higher and use the phone to call in reinforcements if you like, Emma, or do you want us to wait?'

Montana frowned and hesitated and, as she'd hoped, Emma spoke up from where she lay. 'I don't want to think about moving just yet. Can we wait a few minutes, please, Andy?'

'Of course,' Andy said.

'Emma might want to walk herself out, Andy,' Montana said quietly. She smiled at Emma, who was gazing dotingly down at her daughter. 'She looks much better now she's given birth.'

Emma nodded, and Andy looked surprised at how quick she was to seize that idea. 'I can walk now, can't I, Montana? I really don't want a rescue party and my brothers roaring in here. You said women carry their babies to their rooms after giving birth.'

Montana nodded. 'Of course you can, especially with the inducement of a hot shower at the end for the aches and pains.'

'I guess it's not that far.' Andy looked uncomfortable with the idea, though, and Montana grinned.

'Women are pretty tough, Andy.'

'So I have been noticing lately,' Andy acknowledged ruefully.

'Tell me about it,' said Tommy, with awe. 'I wouldn't walk for a week if that happened to me.'

They all laughed and Andy and Montana stepped away to give the new parents time with their daughter.

They climbed the hill a little and watched the moon rise from the east.

'Thank you for arriving on time, Andy. I'll admit to last-minute nerves. I was really glad to see you at the end. It's a bit different if it's someone else who is having the baby in the wilds and not me.'

Andy smiled reminiscently. 'You can say that. I guess I should thank you for the litany in my head as I jogged up here. I kept saying Montana was fine. Emma will be fine.'

She peered up at him in the gathering dark. So solid and calm and wonderful. 'You were just as unruffled and supportive as you were at Dawn's birth. You are an amazing man.'

They turned back, not wanting it to get much

darker before they walked out, if that was what they were going to do. 'Emma is the amazing one. Poor old Tommy will take a while to get over it, I think.'

Andy slipped his fingers around Montana's and covered them with his other hand before he let her go. 'Now all I have to do is capture your heart and we'll be home free.' He turned away and preceded her down the path towards the new parents.

Emma was the first inpatient in the new Lyrebird Lake maternity unit, even though she technically didn't give birth there.

Both sets of grandparents had struggled with the shock of Grace's unexpected birth but had settled down when they'd held the new member of their family.

By nine o'clock that night Montana had decided all the students in town had filed through to see the new baby as well as most of their parents.

Andy shook his head. 'You'd better think about a contraception class on the school bus. It takes an hour to get to the base high school and you'd have a captive audience.'

Montana agreed. 'I'll bring Emma and she can tell them about sleepless nights and crying babies. That should help just as much.'

They both laughed as Sara arrived to take over Emma's care for the night and Andy left Montana to her work.

After an extended handover report, because Sara wanted to know all the details of the bush-baby birth, Montana went in to say goodbye to the new parents.

'It seems you're famous on the school bus,' Montana said, and Emma shook her head.

'Infamous.'

'I think you are amazing.' Tommy stood beside the bed with his new daughter in his arms and stared with awe down at Emma. He turned to Montana. 'How amazing is she?'

'Who? Grace Isobel?' Montana teased, and Tommy looked up in confusion.

'Of course she's amazing, too, but I meant Emma. I could never be as brave as she was today.'

'You did your job, too, Tommy. You three are a family now. Be kind to each other.' She leaned over and kissed Emma's forehead. 'Try and sleep when Grace is asleep. I'll see you tomorrow. It's a big day tomorrow when you take her home.'

'That's scary.'

'Remember, I'll visit every day for the first few days.'

Emma caught Montana's hand. 'Thank you.'

Montana squeezed Emma's hand back and each knew she and this young mum would always be close. 'Thank you, Em. I was the lucky one to be a part of Grace's birth. You were wonderful.' Montana squeezed her hand and smiled. 'Goodnight, you three.'

Montana walked away and she should have been exhausted but she doubted whether she'd be able to relax just yet. It had been a huge day.

As she walked across the grounds towards the house she realised that Andy had waited for her, leaning against a tree.

'Hello, there,' he said, and stood, tall and caring in front of her, and it seemed so right to rest her head against his chest and close her eyes for a second.

'Were you waiting for me?' she mumbled into his shirt.

'It seems to be something I find myself doing a lot of,' he said, and his voice rumbled in his chest under her cheek. Even that vibration was healing to Montana.

'I don't mind,' Andy said. 'It's always worth the wait.'

She stepped back and looked into his face. 'Thank you, dear Andy.'

He took her hand in that way he had of cradling it between both of his and she knew she would always love it when he did that.

They stood there silently for a few minutes before he let her go. 'Would you like to walk around the lake with me for a little while instead of going straight home?'

That sounded like heaven. Just to clear the clutter she'd accumulated from the stresses of the day. 'How did you know?'

'You look a little wired.' She could hear the humour in his voice and it drew an answering smile from her.

'That's an apt description of how I feel.' Already, being with Andy, she'd begun to relax. When he tucked her arm in his and fell into step beside her she knew this was where she wanted to be. By Andy's side. Or in his arms.

They walked in the dark and their eyes became accustomed until they could see their way by reflected starlight off the lake.

The tranquillity seeped back into Montana and she didn't know if it was the peace of their surroundings or the peace of being with Andy. She suspected the latter.

'So are you here to stay?' he asked.

'Yes. To stay,' she said softly, and the conviction in her voice made him tense beside her.

He stopped and turned to face her and she could just make out the planes of his face and the brilliant smile that lit up his face. 'For ever?'

The devotion on his face brought tears to her eyes. How could she have been this fortunate? 'If you'll have me.'

He drew her against him gently as if afraid she'd change her mind. 'I love you, Montana. I've loved you from the first moment on the mountain. I love everything about you and I want to be a part of your and Dawn's lives.'

She squeezed her arms around his waist. 'I love

you, too. I'm sorry I was so slow and fought so hard against falling in love with you. But it didn't do me any good resisting because I do love you. Very much.'

He kissed her gently on the forehead and pulled her against him so she could feel his chest against her. It felt like home.

'You had things to work out. I understood that,' he said into her hair.

She stepped back and tipped her head back to look into his face. 'I think that was what I was afraid of,' she said slowly. 'That I wouldn't be able to separate you and Douglas.'

Her voice strengthened. 'That's not the way it is. I truly loved Douglas, and thought I'd never find love again. And if I hadn't found you then I would have thought I'd loved enough.'

She shook her head as she gazed into his wonderful face. 'I can see that's not true because you are my future and I love you with all my heart. And it will be a wonderful future that we will share together with Dawn.'

He pulled her into his arms and this time when he kissed her there was less patience and more power and a lot more persuasion tightly leashed. Then he kissed her as if she were the most precious gift in the world. 'Marry me. How soon will you be my wife, darling Montana?'

She leaned up and kissed him back. 'As soon as possible, my love.'

Then she smiled mischievously. 'It would be

hard to teach contraception if I was already pregnant before we were married.'

Andy laughed. 'And there is a huge risk of that, let me assure you. We can't let that happen.'

CHAPTER TWELVE

THE wedding was held on the newly built wooden jetty that had been crafted by the townsfolk in only one week. The working party had been led by Emma's dad.

The white railed platform looked out over the water and was the first structure on the beautiful block of land at the end of the lake Andy had bought for the future. Now the future was here.

A laden arch of lavender-coloured roses from Clare's garden adorned the raised temporary stage built so all the townsfolk could see the happy event.

Montana, every inch the bride, was resplendent in a pale ivory gown that whispered against her ankles and bared her shoulders. Her handsome groom stood tall beside her as they listened to the words of the ceremony and every few minutes their gazes would drift towards each other and their smiles excluded the world.

Ned played the bagpipes to lead them out after the service and the strains of the pipes soared gloriously over the water and startled the waterbirds into a swirling formation that should have been doves but it was close enough.

The reception was held in a huge white marquee at the edge of the lake with white-clothed tables and children playing.

Emma, a beautiful bridesmaid in pale lavender to match the roses on the tables, held hands with Tommy, who had a sleeping Grace tucked against his chest in a sling.

They discussed their own wedding the next year and took notes so that it could be as perfect as this one had been.

Andy could feel Montana's hand in his as she talked to his sister, and he could see the smiles and sincerity in the people around him.

He was home. He had his friends and his work. But most of all he had his adorable wife who completed his world in a way he had never imagined would happen.

Montana, too, was at peace. The time ahead was for her and Andy, and for all of Dawn's brothers and sisters to come in the future.

On top of the wedding cake, a gift from Ned, a beautiful silver lyrebird oversaw the festivities.

And later, long after Ned had retired, Montana heard the strains of distant bagpipes drifting out from the bush.